The Three-Legged Turtle

The Three-Legged Turtle

William J. McGillvray

DORRANCE PUBLISHING CO., INC.
PITTSBURGH, PENNSYLVANIA 15222

ISBN # 0-8059-6526-2
Printed in the United States of America

First Printing

For information or to order additional books, please write:
Dorrance Publishing Co., Inc.
701 Smithfield Street
Third Floor
Pittsburgh, Pennsylvania 15222
U.S.A.
1-800-788-7654
Or visit our web site and on-line catalog at www.dorrancepublishing.com

To my wife, Peg, who did a great job
raising three rather crazy individuals.

And to Hugh and Craig,
who made life very interesting, indeed.

Contents

Footprints of today's mighty hunter
Are not in tomorrow's snow.

Chapter One

Stand or Fall

The police were called out for the third time in one week. Another battle had broken out at an employment office of one of the local sawmills. Fistfights would often break out when someone would try to push his way into the line-up. Men and women who had never begged for anything in their whole lives, were now begging on the streets for a measly nickel or a dime. Some of the people who were working could barely put food on the table during the early thirties. There were stories going around that some large families were even selling some of their kids into slavery, so they could feed the rest of the brood. The rumors were never proven, but they persisted for many years.

About the only work available in the province at the time was in the lumber industry. The wages were not high, twenty-five cents an hour was the average, but at least they were wages. In the woods of the Pacific Northwest, it was a time of giant trees and legendary loggers. The Douglas firs were already saplings when the Europeans were just learning to scratch pictures on the walls of their caves.

The best fallers of the day made a dollar an hour and could drive a stake into the ground a hundred feet away from the base of one of these giants, then fall the tree so it landed right on top of the stake. The fallers were the king of the woods and each camp claimed their fallers could fall more trees in the shortest period of time. In the heat of the summer the camps would shut down because of the fire hazard.

That's when all the logging-camp crews headed for the big city. They all had money in their jeans and couldn't wait to blow it on wine, women, and song. The bars and bootleggers would be going night and day when the loggers came to town. The so- called ladies of the night suddenly turned into beauty queens, and as each crew arrived in town it claimed to have men who could out-drink and out-fight any ten cops on the Vancouver police force. Without a doubt the toughest two loggers on the coast were from Cedar Landing, a small logging community just north of Prince Rupert.

Big Ed Cameron and his Indian friend Charley Greywolf could keep the police force occupied for at least two weeks. Invariably, they would wind up in jail maybe two or three times before they finally ran out of money. When their dollars were all gone and they were battered up enough, the court judges would have them put on the boat and shipped back up north.

The small town of Cedar Landing had one general store and two churches. One garage was enough to fix the twenty cars that traveled the five miles of dirt roads that made up the community. There wasn't a hotel with a beer parlor as yet, but that would be added as the population grew and the thirst of the citizens increased. The town itself was small, barely a dot on the map. But the people were all tough, hard-working individuals. You either worked or left town. There just was no place in town for loafers to hang out.

In the spring of 1922, Big Ed's closest friend, Charley, got married to his childhood sweetheart. Vera was beautiful and the only daughter of an old friend of Charley's family. The marriage meant that Big Ed had to go to the city by himself that spring and it was just not the same. He got drunk as a skunk and tried to clear out a beer parlor by himself. The police came storming in with their nightsticks flailing the air and they pounced on poor Ed.

It was a wild melee for sure, and most of the furniture in the place was demolished. One huge Irish cop named O'Malley broke a solid oak chair over poor Ed's head. Poor Ed woke up in the emergency room of the local hospital with a bad concussion, along with a broken jaw, and four cracked ribs. It also took a hundred-odd stitches to stop the bleeding of his many cuts and abrasions. Ed's newest girlfriend, Quennie, ran off with all the money he had left, and his so-called drinking friends absconded with all his luggage. Big Ed arrived back in Cedar Landing looking like he had been run over by a runaway trolley-bus. He swore if he lived to be a hundred years old he would never again be so stupid. Ed always said the same thing after being in the big city for awhile, so no one paid any attention to his vow of abstention.

Big Ed had been home for only three weeks when he met a very pretty lady named Jean Devereaux. Jean was the local mill owner's daughter and she had spent the last four years away at university. She and Ed had not seen each other too often during those years of schooling. Ed had remembered Jean as a little bit flat-chested and certainly nothing to look at. Jean had grown up in more ways than one. It was in the line-up at the town's only grocery store where Ed fell head over heels in love with her. She had accidentally dropped a large roast of beef and Ed picked it up for her.

Jean looked up at the big hunk of a man and liked what she saw. He looked like a strong and rugged individual, that was for sure, but he also had a soft kind look about him. For the first time in his life, Big Ed felt like a tongue-tied teenager. This girl was different than any lady he had ever known. Four months later Jean and Ed were married and the whole town showed up for the party. For a wedding present, Jean's dad loaned them the money to buy the local grocery store. Big Ed made up his mind that night that he was going to quit drinking. He had seen too many good marriages go down the drain because of booze.

One year later Jean presented Ed with a bouncing baby boy; the best kid in the whole world according to Ed. Never in his life had Ed been so completely satisfied with his life. Everything went great for the next three years. Then Jean became ill with cancer, and after being in and out of the hospital for only ten months, she passed away. Ed was absolutely devastated. He felt like his whole world had fallen apart, and if it had not been for his son, Gordon, he would have just walked away from everything. Big Ed had spent his good times raising hell and putting a prop underneath it. Now he spent his darkest of all time in a hell he couldn't deal with. Ed was strong as a horse and nothing had ever got the best of him till now. He sank into a deep well of depression which made suicide seem like a reasonable proposition. If it hadn't been for the long talks with his old friend Charley, he probably would have sought refuge in the bottle.

Charley and his wife, Vera, looked after Ed's young son Gordon as if he was their own. Charley would often say, "There is only one thing wrong with this little buck, he's not Indian." Vera didn't believe in disciplining little ones. She claimed that life has a way of teaching us the lessons we need, and then we never forget them. It has worked great for Vera and Charley's two children, who just happened to be girls. They both grew up to be kind, gentle, and free from any inhibitions.

The system worked fine until Gordon went to school; then Vera's theory broke down badly. The Indian kids seemed to have a built-in respect for the teachers, but not Gordon. He had a built-in hostility toward anyone who told him to sit in one place for more than half an hour. Gordon was now bigger than most of the kids in his class, and their favorite game was to see how many kids it would take to get Gordon on the ground. They would pile on top of Gordy till the sheer weight of numbers would topple him over. By the time he was in seventh grade, there were not enough kids in the school to put Gordy on the ground. The young man was built like his dad and was now just as big and bigger than most of the teachers.

When Gordy was in the seventh grade, he was thirteen years old. One day the principal of the school decided that this young whipper-snapper needed to be taught a lesson that was not in the text books. On that particular day Gordon had been an especial pain in the butt to the entire teaching

3

staff, so he was sent to the principal's office to get the strap. The principal explained to Gordon that it was really for his own good, and that he had no bad feelings toward him. He instructed Gordon to hold out his hand, and then he brought the strap down once, real hard. Gordon looked at the principal straight in the eye and he called him a name that he had seen written on the wall in the boy's toilet. Gordy then hit the principal square on the jaw. The poor principal sagged backwards and landed on his seat. Gordy realized right away that he had made a grave error. He left the school and didn't dare go home. He knew his dad would send him right back to school.

Gordy decided not to go home till things cooled down a bit. He got a lift to Prince Rupert with a logger friend of his dad's. From there he caught a ride to Steveston with a fisherman who also knew his dad. Old Martin, the fisherman, asked Gordy where he was going. Gordy didn't give him any satisfactory answers, so Martin didn't push it any further. He knew that Gordon was a pretty level-headed kid and he had never got into any serious trouble that he had heard about.

Once they reached Steveston and said their goodbyes, it took Gordy an hour to hitch a ride into Vancouver. For the first two nights in the big city he walked the streets all night. It wasn't raining but he was cold, hungry, and miserable. He knew in his gut he should go back home and take his medicine, but he thought he would look like a fool.

On the third day of walking the streets he got talking to another kid called Darcy. This scruffy-looking individual asked him if he were hungry. When Gordy said he was starving, Darcy took him into a restaurant and bought him a meal. After Gordon wolfed down his meal, he asked Gordy if he had a place to sleep. Gordy told him that he had walked the streets for the last three nights. Darcy asked Gordy where he came from and how come he wound up on the street without any money. Then he wanted to know if Gordy had ever been in trouble with the police. When Gordy told him he hadn't, Darcy said he could get him a place to sleep if he wanted. They then got on a streetcar and the scruffy kid took him to an old house somewhere in the suburbs.

Darcy told Gordy to wait outside for a couple of minutes, then he went inside. About ten minutes went by before Darcy came out and got Gordy. The windows were all boarded up and there was only one small light in each room. Gordy figured out right away that these young kids didn't own the old rundown house, and they didn't want any nosey neighbors snooping around. Gordy met the rest of Darcy's gang and they all looked like they could use a good bath.

That same night Gordy started his education in rolling drunks and stealing whatever wasn't nailed down. He didn't think much of this way of life and he also thought the rest of the gang looked like a bunch of losers. The only good thing: It was a lot better than going hungry. Because of his size Gordy got pretty good at rolling the drunks, so the gang agreed to let him stay.

One night the gang got real lucky. They stole ten cases of whiskey out of an old government warehouse. After selling nine of the cases to a bootlegger, it was decided they would have a big party at the old empty house. They were all buddy-buddy to start with, but it wasn't long before two of the young punks got a little too drunk. The two idiots decided to show the new kid who was boss. One of the punks kicked Gordy in the groin when he wasn't looking. His mindless friend pulled out a knife and decided to do some carving on Gordy's torso.

The two tough kids thought they could scare Gordy, but they were dead wrong. He not as drunk as they were and was bigger than either of them. If they had not been all liquored up and trying to act tough, they would have also realized that he was a lot stronger than the two of them put together.

The kid who had first kicked Gordy tried to kick him again, but Gordy saw it coming this time and he grabbed the boy's foot. He yanked so hard that he pulled the kid clean off his feet and down he went, banging his head on the floor. Gordy quickly scrambled to his feet in time to dodge the knife that the second drunken kid jabbed at him. Gordy then hit the skinny punk on the side of the head, and he too dropped like a sack of spuds. Gordy thought, *City kids talk tough and act tough, but one or two at a time they're pushovers.* Gordy also realized he didn't like any of them. He decided that night to move on. He knew if he stayed around this crowd for any length of time, he was going to wind up in jail—and that was one thing he didn't want. Staying in a classroom for five or six hours was torture, but staying in a jail cell for a long time would drive him crazy.

It took Gordy about two hours to hitch a ride to the small town of Hope. In a restaurant he got talking to a truck driver who said he could ride with him to Toronto. It was just what Gordy wanted; getting rides for ten to twenty miles at a time was getting a little boring. The truck driver, Leo, drank beer as he drove and that made Gordy a little nervous. Leo told Gordy that he could drive better when he drank beer; it kept him awake. As he had never driven a truck himself, Gordy didn't really know any better, but he did think it a bit stupid.

Toronto was a lot farther away than Gordy had thought it would be, and as the hours dragged by he began to wonder what he was going to do when he finally got there. One day when they were in the middle of Manitoba, they stopped at a truck stop for a hamburger. Leo asked Gordy if he knew anyone in Toronto he could stay with. When Gordy told him he didn't know a soul in the town, Leo said that his brother-in-law had a small trucking business there and was he always looking for young fellows to swamp on his trucks. He said that he would speak to his brother-in-law and get Gordy some work if he wanted. It would at least tie him over till he found a real good job.

Little did Gordy know that he was going to be working for nothing, that this was a scam the truck driver and his brother-in-law had been working for years. When they finally got to Toronto, Leo took Gordy over and got him the job, as he promised. He then took Gordy to the YMCA, where they gave him a small room. As he was employed at the trucking company, they would allow him to stay till pay day. After three full weeks of working his butt off loading and unloading trucks, Gordy asked the boss of the company for his wages. The boss said he didn't need him anymore and if he came back next Friday, he would pay him.

Gordy told him, "I have to find a place to live and I need the money now."

The boss grunted, "I don't have time right now. Leave the premises now or you won't get anything." With a sinking feeling in his stomach, Gordy walked away. He had been made a fool of and there was absolutely nothing he could do about it. Gordy knew if he went to the police to complain they might just put him in reform school.

Gordy was feeling sick about the whole deal. He knew that he had to go to the hostel and tell them what had happened. The man at the hostel listened intently and said that he was very sorry but there was nothing that they could do. They needed the room. Gordy packed up his few things and said goodbye to the staff. Before he left, one of the men on the staff got Gordy a couple of sandwiches and put them in a bag for him. The man had seen this sort of thing happen many times, to so many young kids.

It was one long, miserable day for Gordy; he finally went to a small park and did a lot of thinking. After eating one of the sandwiches he decided he would leave for home, but first he had to get even with the trucking company boss. Gordy walked around for a few hours, contemplating vengeance against those thieving buggers. At a nearby construction site he found just what he needed: a large spike. When it got dark Gordy climbed the wire fence surrounding the company parking lot. With the spike he had found earlier in the day, Gordy poked several holes in the gas tanks of every truck in the compound. As he was punching the holes, he could imagine the look on the boss's face when he came into work in the morning and realized what had happened. He was tempted to get a match and ignite the gas that was spreading all over the ground. That was stupid, he realized.

After leaving the compound, Gordy kept walking the rest of the night. He wanted to be as far away as possible when the trucking-company boss arrived in the morning. Fearing the boss might send someone to find him, he didn't dare take the main road out of town. After he got lost a couple of times, he finally found an alternate route to the main highway. Gordy managed to get many short rides that first day; one elderly man even stopped to buy him a meal, then insisted he take a twenty-dollar bill. He told Gordy that somebody had done that for him once.

Many times during the next few days, Gordy got so tired and discouraged that he just sat down by the side of the highway. He hadn't realized it was so far to go, that Ontario and Manitoba were so large. At night he would sleep in some farmer's barn or in a granary, and the next morning when he started again the highway would stretch before him like an endless asphalt ribbon. All day he would walk, and yet by nightfall, the countryside looked no different.

Every now and then an old farmer would stop and pick Gordy up. He would let him off after twenty or thirty miles. One really warm day when he was in the middle of Saskatchewan, a police car pulled up just ahead of him. When Gordy saw the police car he thought that maybe he was going to be returned to Toronto to face charges for damaging the trucks. A middle-aged Mountie got out of the police cruiser and walked back to Gordy. He said, "Well young fellow, you look like you're a long way from home. Have you any identification on you?"

Gordy was so tired he could hardly stand up and was swaying from side to side. Finally he said, "My name is Gordon Cameron, and I live in BC. I just didn't think it was so bloody far to walk." He then gave the Mountie his school card. Gordy then volunteered, "I got a ride to Toronto with a truck driver and he got me a job with his rat of a brother-in-law. After working real hard for three weeks, the guy refused to pay me and I had no money for rent or food, so I decided to go home."

The Mountie sighed, then shook his head. "I have some sad news for you, Gordon. There are many people out here in the big world just waiting to take advantage of others who are down on their luck. Hop in the car, Gordon, and I'll see if I can help you get home." It took nearly two hours' driving before they got to Wolsely, the small town where the police station was located. The first thing the Mountie did was to make a fresh pot of coffee. After two cups of the strong brew, Gordon gave Officer Harvey his dad's phone number in Cedar Landing. He was sure his father would be mad as a hatter to receive a call from the police. *He'll think I'm in trouble*, he silently fretted.

Officer Harvey finally came back into the main office and smiled, "Well, Gordon, your dad was glad to hear that you are all right. He's going to wire some money right away to the train station at Indian Head. The train won't be along for another three hours, so we'll go there now. There will be time to have a meal when we get there; how does that sound?" Gordy's rumbling stomach needed no urging. During the hour-and-a-half drive, Officer Harvey asked, "Tell me, Gordon, whatever made you go to Toronto in the first place?"

Gordy hesitated a minute then replied, "Well, it seems kind of a stupid now, but it made a lot of sense at the time. The principal at my school wanted to give me the strap and I didn't think I deserved that. I hadn't really done anything wrong that day. So he strapped me once real hard, and then I hit him on he jaw. I took off and thought they would expel me from the school anyhow, so why wait around? I knew my dad would make me go back and apologize to the principal, and I didn't feel I should."

Officer Harvey looked at the big young man and said, "I'll tell you a little secret, Gordon: Running away doesn't do any good. Because when you do get away, the problem is still there. I also ran away when I was young and I got into a whole pile of trouble. It was only with the help from a lot of good people that I didn't wind up in jail."

When they got to the small community of Indian Head, they went to the train station first and found out that the money from Gordy's dad had arrived. After first buying a train ticket for Gordon, they went to the Main Hotel and had a steak smothered in mushrooms and lots of mashed potatoes swimming in gravy. The steak was about two inches thick and so tender he could cut it with his fork. While they were devouring their meal, Officer Harvey said, "Gordon, you have to stand for something or you will fall for anything. I know it sounds like I'm lecturing, but I know what I'm saying. Whatever you do, don't every waste time blaming someone else for the problems in your life."

The train arrived at last and Gordon climbed on board. He was so happy to be able to sit down for the rest of the journey home. As the wheels clickety-clacked over the rails and the hours rolled by, Gordy did a lot of thinking about what the Mountie had said. He slept like he had not slept for a long time that night. Just the thought of getting back to Cedar Landing and seeing his dad and Charley made him feel so good. The ride through the Rockies was a spectacular panorama of towering snow-capped peaks and plunging valleys; it was an awesome sight.

It had only been two months since he had taken off from Cedar Landing, and now he was going home and it felt so good. Three days later when he got off the water taxi at Cedar Landing, his two-month excursion into the wide world was over for now. Big Ed met Gordy down on the dock and never said boo to him, he just grabbed him and gave him a big hug.

Big Ed's old logger friend, Charley, invited both Ed and Gordy over to his house for dinner that first night. Vera loved cooking and had been well trained in the culinary arts when she was young. She was going to cook up one of her famous stew dinners as a welcome-home dinner for Gordy. Besides the dinner, Charley wanted to hear all about Gordy's adventure in the big world outside. Big Ed looked like he had not slept for a few nights, and he let Gordy know more than once that he was glad he was back. Ed had known that Gordy would take off sooner or later. He had to find out for himself what the big world is like, but his sudden departure had really shattered his composure.

They had a great dinner at Charley's that night, and after the meal Gordy told them all about the trip. He told them about the gang of hoodlums he had been with in Vancouver; how they all got drunk one night and how two of them had attacked him. He even told them about the guy he had worked for in Toronto who wouldn't pay him. He then told them how he had gone back and stuck a spike in the gas tank of the trucks in the company's work yard. He admitted it had been a dumb thing to do.

Gordy also told them about the Mountie who had picked him up somewhere in the middle of the Saskatchewan. He said, "I was so tired by the time the police car arrived that I really didn't think I could walk another step. I had no idea that this country was so big till I started to walk home. The Mountie took me to the police station at Wolsely, where he gave me some strong, fresh coffee before he phoned Dad. He told me two or three times, 'You have to stand for something or you will fall for anything.' He also said more than once that it was a waste of time to blame others. That your life is your fault."

Gordy paused a moment then went on. "Officer Harvey told me that if I can't sit in school all day to do what he did: 'Take the schooling by correspondence courses at your own pace. Get yourself a day job and study at night; that way you will be learning day and night.' I'm sure glad he came along when he did. He also told me that he had done almost the same thing when he was young and nearly got into some very serious trouble. I don't ever remember being as tired as I was when Officer Harvey came by. I really didn't know if I could have walked another hundred yards."

Gordy stopped talking for a minute and looked very thoughtful. Then he said, "You know, I don't think that I want to live in the big cities when I get older. They just don't seem to be the best place to live as far as I can see. Nobody seems to care much for anyone but themselves in the places I saw. So maybe I will just stay where the place is smaller, but the people are bigger. I can't for the life of me figure out why the police let companies like that one I worked for in Toronto stay in business."

Throughout Gordy's whole narration Charley had not said a word. Now he looked over at his old friend Ed, and said, "I think this young buck learned a few great lessons in the last two months. We could have talked to him for years and he would not have learned that much." Ed nodded in agreement and was glad things had worked out the way they had. He hated the thought of the young fellow taking off the way he did. Ed secretly hoped that Gordy might get married to one of the local gals and settle down in Cedar Landing. Then there would be some grandkids he could spoil rotten. Ed had many things to do in the store to keep him busy, but every now and then he got lonely and irritable. The fact that Gordy had came back in one piece helped to calm things down and get them back in their proper prospective.

Chapter Two

Brother of the Bear

"Your Mountie friend was a wise man," said Charley. "He must have been through some big troubles to learn the things he passed on to you. It seems that the great lessons of life come with a very large price tag on them. My young friend, if you are not going to live in the big city then you must learn to be a good hunter. This is a gift you must be taught. If you want I will come over in the morning and we will start your training. The first thing we will do is go out to the old gravel pit, and I will show you how I was taught to shoot a rifle. Maybe when the logging camp starts up in about ten days, we will see if we can get you a job setting chokers. That is, if it is all right with your dad." Ed had been sitting quietly, thinking everything is working out just the way he had always hoped it would. He nodded to Charley; that it was fine with him.

The following morning Charley arrived at Ed's house. Gordy borrowed his dad's hunting rifle and they took off for the gravel pit. At the far end of the old unused gravel pit, Charley put a target up on a post. "Now my young friend, see if you can hit the target," he said. Gordy shot three times and nicked the target once.

"Hmmm," said Charley, "that's pretty good if you plan to scare the animal to death, but let me show you how I do it." He squatted down and rested his left elbow on his left leg, then took aim and shot three times. Each shot went through the bull's-eye. Then Charley looked at Gordy and said, "Remember, never shoot at an animal if it is moving. In the next few weeks I will teach you how to make an animal stop and listen."

On the following morning at five o'clock, Charley was at Ed's house with his backpack on. He and Gordy were going to go for their first hike into the mighty forest of the Rocky Mountains. Charley walked about ten feet ahead and would suddenly stop dead in his tracks, then he would put out his hand to signal Gordy not to make a sound. They would stand motionless for five minutes sometimes; it was eerie. Gordy tried to listen as hard as he could, but all he heard was the odd bird chirping as Charley would stand motionless. All day long they walked deeper into the great green wilderness. It seemed to Gordy like they were being swallowed up in a never ending world of green. For hours they trudged on and on never saying a word. Finally, late in the afternoon, they came to a beautiful quiet lake and Charley decided to pitch camp.

After their six-hour hike they were both hungry as a bull-moose, so old Charley cooked them up a good meal. They sat and drank tea for a long time, while Charley explained about the sounds they had heard that day. Each sound apparently meant something different, and Charley could imitate every sound. A loon called out from across the lake and Charley held his breath. "That my young friend, is the most spiritual sound in all of nature. It tells the experienced hunter that all is well with the world. It is said that only those with a quiet heart can hear that beautiful sound. Legend has it that the loon heard that sound from an Indian princess who had lost her brave in battle, the day before their wedding.

"To be a truly great hunter you must know the animal that you hunt, just like you know your own brother. Remember, the Great Spirit loves the animals of the forest as much as he loves the hunter. A mighty hunter must have a quiet heart, my young friend." After a long pause, Charley continued, "Tomorrow we will hear more of our forest friends." For almost two weeks they trudged the valleys and the hills where mighty hunters had roamed, long before the white man had ever been seen in these parts.

The boss at the logging camp was an old friend of Ed and Charley's, and after looking over the strong young man, he agreed to start Gordon setting chokers the next day. He said he would keep an eye on Gordy for the first couple of weeks, because the older loggers loved to give the young green-horns a tough time. Gordy worked as hard and fast as he could. When the older loggers tried to get his goat, he would just laugh at them. Gordy kept thinking, *Just you wait, you old farts, one day I'll work you into the ground.*

Each night after a hard days' work and a huge meal of steak and all the fixin's, he would take his dad's rifle out to the gravel pit and fire off a box of shells. Sometimes Charley would go with him and they would have a contest. Gordy's eyes were much younger so he usually won the contest. When the logging camp would shut down for any reason, Charley and Gordy used that time to go hiking into the Headless Valley, or the Mountains of the Moon. Charley had his special names for every region for hundreds of miles around, according to the old Indian legends. Charley had taught Gordy how to snare rabbits and catch fish, and by the time he had the tent up and the fire lit, Gordy would be back with the dinner.

One day Charley told Gordy, "Remember, my young man, that all animals are curious; they have to be. If you can learn to make a bird call or an animal noise, any animal will stop to listen. To our furry friends, any noise may be a meal moving around in the underbrush or it may be a warning call, so they all stop to listen. That is when you shoot your prey, never when it is moving. A wounded fox has been known to kill a man."

When they would get back from the woods, Gordy would go back to work in the logging camp. By the time he was seventeen years old, he was given a job as a faller. When he was twenty-three years old, Gordy could swing a broad-axe from early morning till nightfall. He had arms like trees and sinews like the chokers they used. The young fellow seemed tireless, and many of the older loggers had stopped trying to keep up to him. Charley and Gordy went hunting late one September. It had been extremely hot that summer and all the logging camps had all shut down for fire season. The year was 1939, and the Second World War had just broken out. Gordy knew that he would have to go and do his part. He felt odd whenever someone told him of a young fellow half his size who had already joined up. He had been taught early in life that you don't let others carry your load.

It was hot as Hades in the woods, and at times great swarms of mosquitoes nearly drove the two men nuts. One night while they were sitting by the fire drinking tea, Charley told Gordy stories about some of the great hunters and legendary warriors among his ancestors. He had taught Gordy how to tell a mighty story and when to stop, which was just as important. Many times old Charley would say, "The telling of the hunt will last long after the taste of the meat has been forgotten.

"I have a feeling you will leave us soon my young friend," said Charley. "You are like a son to my wife and to myself. You have let me teach you all the hunting skills my father taught me, the skills die if you do not pass them on. Because we had two girls, the things I learned from my father, who also was a mighty hunter, were coming to an end. As Chief of the Bear Clan, I am going to make you a 'Brother of the Bear.' From now till the Great Spirit says so, you will be protected by the Bear. Vera and I will miss you, my young friend."

That particular night Gordy did not sleep very well. He wondered how he was going to break the news to his dad that he was going to join the army. He wished his father would get involved with some of the local ladies. There were a couple of unattached women around the town but they didn't seem to interest Ed. If his dad only had a lady friend to keep him company, Gordy wouldn't feel so bad about leaving him. It was late when Gordy finally dozed into a fitful sleep.

The next day when they were having their third cup of morning coffee, Gordon brought up the subject. Charley laughed quietly, then said, "Your dad has a lady friend but he didn't want you to know, because he thought you might be hurt. Ed loved your mother more than any man ever loved a woman, and he loves you too. He didn't want you to think he was being unfaithful to your mother's memory. So my young friend, the Great Spirit is taking care of everything. You have to go and travel your own journey, it will be very interesting, believe me."

Chapter Three

Merchant Navy

A few days later Charley talked to his old friend Big Ed, and he told Ed that Gordon was planning to leave soon to join the army. "He didn't actually says he was leaving on any certain date, but I figured that it will be soon." Big Ed knew that Gordy had wanted to say something for the last week, but didn't know how to say it. Ed just waited and didn't want to broach the subject; he hoped something would happen to make Gordy change his mind. As usual Gordy went to the Saturday night dance at the school house. All the young bucks and fillies turned up and hoped to make a connection with someone of the opposite sex. Ed wanted Gordy to meet some young local girl and maybe decide to stay around a while longer, but it didn't work out that way. It worked out exactly the opposite. The young fellows at the dance were talking about the war and how they were gong to join up as soon as they could. Some of the young men seemed jealous of the two young men who had already left. Time seems to drag its butt at times when you're young, and these healthy young bucks wanted to get into the action in the worst way.

A week and a half after Charley and Gordy got home from their hunt, Gordon told his dad that the time had come for him to go and join the army. He named the two young fellows who had already left, and both of them were younger than he was. Gordy expected his dad to put up some kind of argument. He really didn't want to hurt his dad's feelings, but he felt like it was the time to go. Gordy was wrong and surprised at the same time—Ed didn't argue a bit.

If Charley had not told him that Gordy was thinking of leaving, it would have been a shock. Ed said, "I knew you would eventually go, son; I just hoped it would be much later. This stupid war is liable to go on for a few years, you know. They haven't even started shooting at each other yet, so there is really no great hurry. Anyway Gordon, you will do what you think you should do and I will respect your decision. Just promise me that you won't do anything stupid." His dad's response to the news that he was leaving took the wind out of Gordy's sails; maybe he was being too rash.

Gordy didn't know what to say at first. He knew darn well his dad was right and that there was plenty of time to enlist. Gordy felt his friends would think he was a slacker if he let others do his fighting. After all, he was a lot bigger and stronger than the two fellows who had already joined up. Ever since he was a kid, Gordy had been told that you always help your neighbor and you don't wait around till the dirty work is all done. Ed knew in his heart that Gordon had to go; he was just too bloody big to hide. If he were a few years younger, Ed would be going himself. The kid was only doing what he had been told a thousand times over. Ed felt very sad now that he knew that Gordy was actually going; they were getting along so well.

Ed said, "Will you do me one more big favor, Gordon? I suppose you plan to go down to Vancouver to join up. When you get there, will you please go see your Aunt Hazel, first thing. Your Aunt Hazel thinks the world of you, son, and you haven't seen her for two or three years, at least. I know your aunt gets very lonely since her husband, Alvin, died. I should write her once in a while, but you know how I am at writing letters. That's all I ask of you, Gordon. She would be tickled to death to see you again. You could take her out for dinner at a nice restaurant, she doesn't get out that often and I know she would love it."

Gordy left Cedar Landing the following morning and he arrived in Vancouver at three-thirty in the afternoon. He wanted to have a couple of beers first off, then maybe see if he could meet some little doll who was lonely for some company. But he had promised his dad he would go and see his Aunt Hazel and take her out for dinner. It was sure not his idea of a big night on the town, going to see some rickety old aunt. He would phone his aunt up and let the phone ring twice, then hang up real fast. Then he could tell his dad that he had phoned her up and there was no one home. Gordy dialed his Aunt Hazel's number as he promised he would, but she picked up the phone on the first ring. Aunt Hazel had the phone right beside her favorite chair, and she was not only in, but she wanted Gordy to come right over. The dear old thing promised Gordy that she would make him a nice hot cup of tea when he got there. *What the hell,* he thought, *one more day is not going to make any difference.*

When he arrived at his dear old aunt's apartment, she was so pleased to see him and made such a fuss about him coming to see her that he felt like a bit of a heel for thinking that it was a waste of time seeing his dear old aunt. Gordy didn't say anything about promising his dad that he would come and see her. He let her think it was all his idea. *What the heck*, he thought, *what she doesn't know won't hurt her.*

Later they went out to a good nearby restaurant and had a very nice meal and a lot of laughs. Gordy could make her laugh easily, and he realized she really was a dear old thing who did think the world of her big, good-looking nephew. During the conversation at dinner, he mentioned that he was going to join the army. Aunt Hazel looked a bit startled all of a sudden. Her late husband, Alvin, had been in the army in the First World War and he had been very badly wounded. For the next twenty-odd years Alvin spent at least four months out of every year going in and out of military hospitals.

Gordy had noticed the startled look on his aunt's face, and he asked her what was the matter. Hazel said, "I wish you wouldn't join the army, Gordon. Your Uncle Alvin spent nearly his whole life as an invalid because of being in the army." Hazel waited a few minutes so that what she said had just said could sink in. Then she said, "Why don't you join the Merchant Navy, Gordon? I have a very dear friend of mine who works at the manning pool. He has often told me that they need young men in the worst way. My friend, Mr. Carlson, claims they pay real well and the food is the best there is. Why don't you stay at my place tonight, and I'll phone Mr. Carlson in the morning and see what he says?"

Gordy thought, *Nuts to the army*, as soon as he heard the words "good food." At nine o'clock the following morning Gordy's aunt phoned up her gentleman friend, Mr. Carlson, at the Merchant Navy manning pool. When he finally came to the phone, Hazel told him about her young nephew and how he was planning to join the army. She suggested that he join the Merchant Navy and he seemed quite interested. Mr. Carlson paused a moment then said, "Bring the young man down to the manning pool about eleven o'clock, but as he doesn't have any sea time, so I don't know if I can place him." Mr. Carlson always said that to cover his own butt.

The following morning, Gordy took his aunt out for breakfast. When she gave her order to the waitress, he nearly burst out laughing. She ordered a bit of dry toast with a cup of tea. Gordy commented, "Aren't you going to have anything else to eat? I have seen some dickey birds that eat more than that for breakfast." Gordy had six large pancakes and a half-dozen fried eggs with about a dozen pieces of bacon on the side. He still didn't feel full but he figured he'd last till lunch time.

At eleven o'clock Gordy and his aunt walked into the manning-pool lobby, and all the girls in the big office looked up and smiled their sexiest smiles. Gordy was a real good-looking young man with wide shoulders. The two hundred and fifteen pounds of muscle on his carcass was spread all over his large frame. His shirt was open at the neck and the hair on his chest tumbled out in disarray. Gordy's short sleeves also revealed powerful arms that had done a lot of hard work in their time.

The young ladies in the office usually saw only old beat up winos and men who had been turned down by the other services coming in as their recruits. Or sometimes, an irate father would bring down his pimply faced kid hoping the Merchant Navy would take the lad and make a man out of him. The office girls nearly fell over each other trying to sign up Gordy. In five minutes flat, his seaman's papers were typed up and his picture pasted on his ID card.

He was also issued a meal pass for the dining room and assigned a room on the second floor of the old Dunsmuir Hotel. Gordy was then told that he would get paid seaman's wages while he waited to be signed on a ship. He thought, *This has got to be my lucky day*, this was more than he even hoped for. Gordy felt so good about everything, that he insisted on taking his Aunt Hazel out to lunch. Then he took her home in a taxi and thanked her again. He promised the dear old thing that he would phone her up in a couple of days and let her know what was happening. Gordy then went out for his long- awaited couple of beers. He did meet a sweet little Irish girl who was down on her luck. He changed Bridget's luck and sent the little darling home, happy as a June bride.

When the people running the manning pool realized how many groceries Gordy could stow away in one day, they held an emergency meeting of the staff and the cooks. The administrators decided they had better get Gordy a berth on a ship as quickly as possible, or some of their clientele would be on short rations before long. After all, they reasoned, their budget was only so big and the war could last for years. So they juggled around a lot of names, and in eight days they had Gordy signed on a nearly new oil tanker running down to Valparaiso, Chile. The first trip was a little bit hectic for Gordy. Some of the crew who had a little sea time under their belts liked to show off by giving the green hands a bad time. Gordy didn't let them get his goat though, and they realized he was a little too big and a little too strong to fool around with. He soon caught on to one fact of shipboard life, get in good with the cook and you have it made.

Dan, the ship's cook, was an ornery little character who had been cooking on freighters for years. He was a pretty good cook, but he definitely had a personality problem. None of the crew liked him much or ever wanted to go ashore with him. Some members of the crew liked to beat the tar out of the poor little runt if they caught him ashore by himself. No one would dare lay a hand on the cook if he was with Gordy. One of the ship's crew did give the cook a bad time once when Gordy was there, and regretted it.

The little senoritas in Valparaiso loved the big Canadian because he was kind, generous, and a lot of fun. They would dance and drink the night away, and sometimes Gordy would take one of the dolls for a stroll in the moonlight. Then the cook would be alone for a while, hoping and praying that none of the crew would come by. After two trips on the oil tanker,

Gordy signed off and went back into the manning pool. He could see that a person could easily get trapped on a run like that and he wanted to see some other places. After being back in the manning pool for a week, he decided to go to Cedar Landing to see his dad and Charley. When he got back to the manning pool, he was signed on an old ship heading for Cochin, India.

The trip to India on this old rust-bucket was plagued with a lot of minor breakdowns. The cargo of wheat was finally unloaded in Cochin, and then the ship was sent to Cape Town, South Africa. When they were a week out of Cochin, the bosun became very sick, so they gave his job to Gordy on a temporary basis. Some of the crew bitched a little because they had more sea time than Gordy, but as it was only going to be temporary, they let it slide. Most of the crew liked the big fellow because he was so easy to get along with. But as usual, there was one fly in the ointment.

There was one loudmouthed snook among the crew who thought he should have on the bosun's job. This skinny, miserable little character acted like a seagoing lawyer, and of course he knew all the union rules and regulations. The scrawny little guy wanted to call a strike, but he couldn't get the crew to back him up. Gordy decided he had better go talk to this little squirt and get this situation straightened out. But the man just would not listen. He just yelled and hollered obscenities at Gordy. Anybody in his right mind would know that was not a smart thing to do.

Gordy grabbed the puny little runt by his shirt front and hoisted him over the side of the ship. They were a good thousand miles from land in all directions and the poor guy knew it. The fellow turned white as a ghost, and after five minutes Gordy lifted him back aboard ship. Never again did he argue with the bosun. When Gordy spoke, no matter how quietly, the guy jumped. It was a once-in-a-lifetime learning experience for them both. The seagoing lawyer learned to never swear at the bosun, and Gordy learned that people who can't swim get very scared when they are held over the side of a ship.

The ship was sailing empty at the time and bouncing around like a ping-pong ball. The wind suddenly got worse and was soon blowing just below hurricane level. For ten solid days the wind howled through the rigging and the crew had a very bad time. The propeller would come out of the water every couple of minutes and would nearly shake the old tub apart. The engine room of a ship is a hot, smelly, miserable place to be in even in good weather. But in real heavy seas, just standing up trying to read the water level in the boilers can be difficult.

The poor cook was also having his troubles. He couldn't keep the pots on the stove, even with an extra man in the galley. None of the crew got enough sleep and they were getting bitchier and more irritable by the day. The nerves of some of the crew members were so frazzled and edgy, you had to be careful how you looked at them. The officer on watch, had to break up more than one argument between old shipmates before it came to blows.

There was one old Liverpool Irishman on board called Paddy, and this poor old rum-dumb character didn't have both oars in the water. For some reason Paddy would lose his concentration every few minutes. Everyone figured he had drank too much booze for too long a time. The officers tried to keep old Paddy off the helm when they were in a storm or coming into or leaving a port. For some reason old Paddy was on the wheel at one point in this storm and he drifted off into his dream world. Paddy let the ship swing to starboard. The ship caught one gigantic wave almost broadside. That one wave wiped all the life rafts and lifeboats off the port side of the ship. One real skinny crew member was nearly washed overboard. The poor guy got jammed in between two steel uprights, and that was all that saved his bacon. It took four crew members nearly an hour to free the poor fellow; he was badly bruised but otherwise unhurt. On the tenth day the clouds broke up and the wind finally died down.

Surviving a real bad storm at sea leaves the crew nearly euphoric because everyone on board is so glad to have survived the continual battering. The ship stayed in Cape Town for an extra three days to give the crew more time to repair some of the damage. By the time they set sail again the ship was in pretty good shape. It's an ill wind that doesn't bring some good to someone. Thanks to the horrendous storm, Gordy had gained years of experience in a very short time.

After taking on a cargo of copra in the Belgian Congo, the ship took off across the South Atlantic. At that particular time in the South Atlantic, the German Navy had a new gimmick they were trying out. The Germans disguised some of their smaller battleships as freighters. The ships would fly a neutral flag and sail to within firing range of their six-inch deck guns. Then they would run up the German ensign, just before they lowered the artificial bulkheads. It was far too late for the Allied freighters to get out of range and they would be blasted out of the water. It was a nasty piece of work they had to admit, but it worked well for a time. Eventually the Allied ships started to report all ships and their location to the British Navy. It didn't take long before all the phony freighters were caught or sunk.

When the ship eventually got back to Vancouver, Gordy again signed into the manning pool. He felt a great need to be on solid ground for a little while, so he went back to Cedar Landing for a bit of a holiday. Old Charley, Gordy, and Ed went hiking for a couple of days into the quietness of the deep woods. It was great, thought Gordy, having his dad along this time. They would sit at night beside a campfire and talk for hours on end. Gordy would tell them about the places he had been and the things he had learned. Ed and Charley would sit quietly and be amazed at the exploits of the young fellow. After five days Gordy found it harder to sit in one place. He had a strong feeling that he needed to be somewhere else; he didn't know why, he just had to go. On the sixth day he said his goodbyes and left to go back to the manning pool.

When he got back to the pool they had another ship waiting for Gordy. It too was an older ship; a real old bucket of bolts that had been under repairs for the last six months. Anything that could float and carry cargo was being used at this stage of the war. Gordy was signed on as a bosun this time and that meant there was no one squawking or trying to get his job. The rest of the crew had already been signed on. They were an odd bunch of characters, but at least they had been to sea before. They were from about five different countries and that was all right with Gordy, as long as they spoke some form of English. The stores were brought on board and the old bucket of bolts was finally ready to sail. Their destination was the South Sea Island of New Britain.

After the ship left Hawaii, the lack of air vents and fans on the old tub became apparent. The trip through the tropics was extremely hot, but otherwise uneventful. In thirty-two days the ship arrived at its destination. The Australian Army garrison at Rabaul had not been notified of the ship's arrival. With their heavy-caliber naval gun, they fired two shots across the bow of the old tub. The officers on the bridge started running around like a gaggle of mad hens, trying to get the right flags up the mast. Finally they were given the signal to proceed into the port.

Many years before, the Island of New Britain had been called the garden spot of the Pacific. Then a whole series of volcanic eruptions and earthquakes changed the atmosphere of the place. One real bad volcano had buried a village and killed everyone there. The thin plumes of smoke and ash from two smaller volcanoes covered the countryside with a thin layer of gray pumice. It was good for the vegetation but not very good for the lungs of the inhabitants.

Chapter Four

Sister Gail

It took a full three weeks to load the ship's holds with copra. Then they were ordered to put a deck load of hardwood on board. By the time they had all the timbers piled on the decks, the great heavy cants were piled twelve feet high. The captain complained about the deck load being too high for such an old ship, but the main office claimed they had clearance from the insurance company, so there was nothing the captain could do but pile it on. Gordy was put in charge of loading the massive hardwood timbers on number three hatch. This was a lot like loading timbers on railway flat car in a logging camp, only they weighed a lot more.

Gordy was amazed at how well things were going on his hatch. Maybe things went too well and he got a little careless. When there were only two more sling loads of timbers to pile on the hatch, one of the slings broke. A great hardwood timber came crashing down on Gordy's left foot. He was told later that the howl he let out could be heard throughout the whole Bismarck Archipelago. It took the crew a good twenty minutes to free Gordy's left foot from under the huge cant.

It was the next afternoon before Gordy woke up in bed in the Rabaul General Hospital. He slowly opened one eye and looked around the room, then he opened up the other eye. He found himself looking into a pair of the biggest, most beautiful brown eyes he had ever seen in his whole life. Gordy looked at this small person in the white veil and gorgeous eyes as though he wanted to eat her. He asked, "Where am I, and what part of heaven did you come from, little one?"

The nursing sister said, "You are in the Rabaul General Hospital, Mr. Cameron. You injured your left foot yesterday on that ship which is at the dock. I'm afraid if you had not been wearing those heavy safety boots, I doubt if the doctor could have saved your foot. The doctor took an hour just getting your boot off. Apparently there were some bones broken, but the doctor thinks your foot will mend if you don't put any weight on it. You must lay very still and don't try to get out of bed, whatever you do."

Gordy looked at the cute little nurse and said, "What is your name, little one? I just know I'm going to need a lot of special care and I would sure like to know your first name."

The perky little nurse gave Gordy a businesslike look and replied, "I will call you Mr. Cameron, all right, and you will call me Sister Gail. If you can remember to do that, we will get on just fine." Then the nurse asked Gordy, "Where are you from, Mister Cameron? Are you an American?"

Gordy looked intently at the little nurse and smiled, "No, Sister Gail, I'm a Canadian and my first name is Gordy, so why don't you tell me your first name?" Sister Gail looked over at Gordy for a minute and thought, *This big bloke sure is not bashful.* She went over and straightened his bed once more. Just for a minute she thought he was going to grab her. She felt her face flush and her heart miss about two fast beats. An hour after Sister Gail left the room, a small Filipino doctor came in to see Gordy.

"My name is Dr. Alverez, and I took care of you when they brought you in yesterday. Some small bones were fractured, but they were clean breaks and should mend nicely, if you stay off your foot!" Dr. Alverez continued, "I think it best that you remain here for the next three weeks, and then you will be sent to the main hospital in Sydney. Barring any complications, your foot should be as good as new in about three months, but you must not put any weight on it."

The next day three members of the ship's crew came to see Gordy in the hospital. They told him that the new bosun was a bit of a prune. He felt real bad when they left. Captain Shurwood and the first mate, Mr. Lyons, came to visit later that day. After a few questions about how Gordy felt, the captain said, "The ship is ready to sail Cameron, and I'm afraid we have to leave at eight bells. The main office in Sydney had been told of the accident and they will take care of all your bills, don't worry about that. All of your belongings have been packed and they will be brought to the hospital before we leave."

Gordy could see that the captain was feeling uncomfortable and would probably leave any time, so he said, "Tell me captain, is there any rule that you couldn't take me back home as a passenger. I won't be doing anything but lying in a bed if I stay here, why can't I just lie down on a ship's bunk?" The captain looked at the mate for a minute then said, "There is a small problem, Cameron. We don't have a doctor on board. If anything happened to your foot while we were at sea, you might just live to regret it. I don't think the main office would think it was a very smart idea. I could send them a wire and see what they say if you want," said the captain. "I'll get Mr. Lyons to send a wire to Sydney when we leave and there should be an answer before the day is out."

As the captain and the mate left, Gordy was feeling like he had just gotten a reprieve from a fate worse than death. The next three hours dragged by like weeks long. Then Sister Gail came into the room with an envelope on a tray and she gave it to Gordy; then she went about her business. She didn't waste any time in the room and seemed to be very detached all of a sudden. Gordy wondered what was eating her.

Gordy opened the envelope and it said, "The insurance company will not pay for a sick passenger, unless the ship has a proper doctor. Sorry, Mr. Cameron will have to stay in the hospital." The statement also said, "Mr. Cameron's wages will be paid in full, until the doctors in Sydney say his foot is fully healed." There was a small note scribbled onto the bottom piece of paper and it was from the first mate. It said, "You did a good job, Cameron, hope we will sail together again." Gordy was suddenly feeling as though he was being discarded like a broken piece of machinery.

Gordy suddenly felt the urge to get out of the bed and to hell with the blasted foot. *Of all the rotten luck*, he thought. He remembered looking at all the slings before they started loading that morning, and they were all in good shape. Why would that one break? He wondered if one of the crew had tampered with it. Gordy also couldn't figure out why they wouldn't take him back as a passenger. He only had a broken foot, after all, not a heart attack or a stroke.

Sister Gail happened to come into the room at that moment with some medicine for Gordy. She knew right away that something was definitely wrong because she could actually feel the anger in the room. The big Canadian certainly wasn't smiling this time, and she thought that maybe he was mad at her. Sister Gail said, "Well, Mr. Cameron, I can see that you are not smiling now. What happened, some other sister wouldn't give you her name?" As soon as she had the words out of her mouth, Sister Gail knew that it was the wrong thing to say.

Gordy looked at her and said, quite emphatically, "No, Sister Gail, I am angry because my ship is leaving Rabaul today, and I am stuck in this blasted place!"

Sister Gail left the room in a hurry and walked to the desk at the far end of the ward. The other nurse on duty was writing up some papers when her friend arrived at the desk. Sister Perrin looked up and asked, "What is the matter, love? Blimey, you look like you have just run over your pet wallaby."

"You wouldn't believe what I have just done, so help me. I have just done the dumbest thing I have ever done in my entire life," said Sister Gail.

Then she told her friend Perrin what happened in the Canadian's room. She said, "What an awful ruddy thing to say to a patient! I don't know what I can do to make it up to him, so help me!" Perrin could see that Kellie was really shaken up by her foolish remark.

Sister Perrin looked at her longtime nursing friend. She smiled and wondered what this bloke was like. Perrin had seen Kellie Gail get out of numerous scuffles with a lot of so-called fast operators. This bloke, whoever he was, sure had her friend in a dither that was for sure, and Kellie Gail didn't get upset very easily. She had seen Kellie in some pretty dicey situations and she had come out unscathed.

"Watch the desk, will you love? I have to go down and take a peek at this bloke that has you so frazzled." With that, she was away like a gust of wind. Sister Perrin casually entered Gordy's room, picked up the chart from the hook at the end of the bed, and looked it over. Then Perrin put the chart back on its hook and took a good look at Gordy. "Well Mr. Cameron, how are you today; is there anything you need? Is your foot giving you any discomfort at all? By the way, I want to tell you that Sister Gail is very upset at what she said to you a few minutes ago. She wants you to know that she is sorry for her remark."

Gordy replied, "Will you do me a favor? Tell Sister Gail for me, that it was not her I was mad at. She is a very beautiful girl and I like her a lot. I would never do anything to upset her, believe me. By the way, could you tell me her first name?"

Sister Perrin hesitated a moment then said, "It is Kellie, but please don't call her that when the other staff are around. We are not really supposed to get that friendly with patients. Nursing rules, you know." Sister Perrin left the room and hurried back to the desk. Her friend Kellie was still standing at the desk, doing her own report, when Perrin returned. She said to Kellie, "That Canadian bloke is really something out of the box, love, and to tell you the truth, I think he likes you a lot. He told me that he is not mad at you. I don't think there is anything you could do that would make him angry. Why don't you go down there right now and try to cheer him up?"

Kellie went down the hall and into Gordy's room once more. She straightened up his bed once again, then she filled his water jug, even though it was still half full. She moved the chair over a bit and adjusted the drapes a couple of times; then she asked him if he wanted his bed up higher, or lower. After Kellie had turned Gordy's pillow a couple more times, she asked if there was anything else she could do for him. She knew that he watched every move she made, and it made her nervous. *Why do I let this big gorilla bother me? He's really not different than any of the other bozos. Why does every blasted male who comes into a ruddy hospital try to make a play with the nurses? This ruddy big overgrown bozo is no different, blast him anyway.*

That night after Kellie got off shift, she and Perrin went to visit some friends they knew in town. They often visited this young couple after a long day in the hospital. The young man, Robert, worked for the Australian government, and he and his wife were about their age. It was a good break from always associating with medical people. An hour after they arrived, Kellie decided to go back to the hospital and turn in. It had been a very stressful day.

Perrin decided that she would go back with her friend, and soon Kellie was talking about the big Canadian. Perrin didn't say anything, but she knew Kellie was not quite as free and easy-going as she was, even a week ago. Just before they reached the hospital Perrin said, "Kellie, why are we discussing Mr. Cameron? I don't think his medical problem is quite that complicated that we have to talk about him all the time."

Kellie looked over at her friend and started to laugh. Kellie said, "What do you think I should do Perrin? The big bozo is starting to get on my nerves, fair dinkum!"

Perrin thought for a minute, then she said, "The Canadian will be going to Sydney pretty soon, am I not right? Why don't you wait and see what he does when he gets well. If you don't hear from him anymore, then you'll know he really didn't care that much."

Early the next morning Kellie went into Gordy's room. She put on her strictly business façade and didn't say a thing. She had not slept very well the previous night and was a little irritated with herself. Gordy watched her carefully but kept quiet; he felt that his little nurse was not feeling very friendly. Gordy messed up his bed a bit and asked her to straighten it up before she left. Kellie came over and tucked in his sheets again. He looked her right in her big, beautiful brown eyes and whispered, "Kellie, if I told you that you have a cute little figure, would you hold it against me?"

Kellie couldn't believe her ears for a minute. She said, "You're going to be here for the next three weeks, Mr. Cameron. You might as well learn to relax. You can't walk on that foot no matter what, or it won't heal."

Gordy looked at her and smiled. He knew he was bothering her and thought it amusing. He said, "I'm relaxed, little one, but I will need a lot of extra attention." Sister Gail left the room again, feeling that the big bozo had got the best of her once more.

The next three weeks went by fast, and the rest of the nursing staff were quite amused at the amount of time Sister Gail was spending in the big Canadian's room. His was the first room she did in the morning and the last one at night. The day arrived when Gordy was to be flown to Sydney to finish his convalescence. When the ambulance came to take Gordy to the airport, Sister Gail volunteered to travel to the airport with the patient. On the way Gordy told Kellie, "Now listen, little one, I'm going to write to you every couple of days and I hope you will write back. I would just hate to have to report you to the Nurses Association for being cruel and inhumane to a poor sick patient." They went over a couple of the many potholes in the road, and Gordy nearly fell off the little bench he was lying on. Kellie reached over to hold him down, and he grabbed her ever so gently and gave her a big kiss. Then he looked at her and gave her another nice long kiss.

Kellie straightened up and said, "Mr. Cameron! I don't know if you know it or not, but it is against the rules to kiss a nurse while she is on duty. I just might have to report this whole incident to my superior if it happens too many times." They both laughed.

The blasted ambulance got to the airport before any more incidents had time to occur. Gordy was wishing the airport was another twenty miles away. He thought, *No telling what could happen on another twenty miles of this bumpy road.*

As the small plane took off for Sydney, Gordy knew deep inside that he would have to see Kellie again, come hell or high water. He never had much trouble getting on with the ladies, but this little dinkum Aussie was different. Gordy didn't know if would he have believed it if someone had told him, that they would meet again and nearly die together.

Chapter Five

Back to Rabaul

Gordy was a patient in the Sydney General Hospital for the first full month, and then he spent another month in an outpatients' residence. With the physiotherapy and a lot of hard work on his part, his foot was eventually as good as new. He wrote to Kellie about once a week, but the mails were so erratic to the islands that he was getting a little downhearted. Kellie wasn't getting half of Gordy's mail, and he was getting even less of hers. He didn't know for sure whether she wanted to hear from him or not. The truth was that a lot of the mail was being diverted to another island first, and then getting lost in transit.

The war in the Pacific had started while Gordy was in the hospital and it was going badly. The Japanese forces were getting closer to Australia every day. The news always kept getting worse, never any better. The Australian government was raising a big stink in London. The regular Australian Army was overseas in Burma and North Africa, when it was really needed at home in the worst way. One day a small Japanese submarine ran aground in Sydney harbor. That really shook up the population and caused an uproar.

Gordy phoned up the Nurses Association and tried to find out about the nurses on New Britain. The operator made him wait ten minutes, then claimed it was classified information and they wouldn't tell him a thing. He also knew the army wouldn't tell him the day of the week for the same reason. One night just after Gordy got out of the medical residence, he met an Aussie soldier in a pub. This soldier claimed that he had been stationed at Rabaul, just two weeks previous. He told Gordy all the soldiers on the island had been brought back to defend the mainland, and as far as he knew, all the white people on the whole island had been evacuated.

Gordy asked him, "What happened to the white nurses at the Rabaul hospital; do you know if they brought out the nurses too?"

The soldier said he really didn't know, but his captain might know, so he left the table and went to a phone. When the soldier came back he said, "The captain didn't know for sure, but said there were some white nurses on the same ship he came back on. If the nurses were white they were probably taken home, but he wouldn't bet on it. The only ruddy way you will ever find out is by going to Darwin. These people down here won't tell a bloke the time of day even if they know it." He said, "If you decide to go to Darwin, see Captain Denny. He is one fair dinkum bloke and if anyone can help you, the captain will be your best bet. If you do get to Darwin and see him, tell him Sergeant Heck sent you."

Early the next day, Gordy went down the airline office at Kingsford Airport. There were not too many people booking flights to Darwin these days, so the office was anything but crowded. The brand-new clerk behind the counter was a young fellow named Teddy. He was a skinny little runt who had just started the job. He thought it would be a real good idea to show his new boss that he could handle authority as well as anyone. Teddy forgot there are good days to exercise authority and there are bad days to exercise authority, and this was definitely a bad day.

The little clerk took a deep breath and asked the big bloke on the other side of the counter, "Exactly why do you want to go to Darwin, sir? If you had read the paper lately, sir, you would know that there will be a state of emergency declared in Darwin next week? I strongly suggest that you wait till next week and get some clearance from the army, and then come back."

Gordy was not looking forward to the long flight to Darwin and he was not in any mood for games. He looked at the little squirt behind the counter for a minute, then he reached across the counter and grabbed him by the shirt front. He seemed to be a giant to the little ticket seller. Gordy scowled as he said, "Tell me friend, do you have a flight to Darwin or not? If you do have a flight, please make out a ticket and I'll pay you now."

Teddy quickly made out the ticket and his voice was quivering as he said, "Thank you sir, I hope you enjoy your flight." Teddy then told the boss that he was not feeling very well, and would have to go home for the rest of the day. He had worked in a petrol station for a long time and thought that this would be a much easier job. Nobody told him when he applied for the job that every once in a while a big bloke would be pulling him over the counter and demanding some instant service.

The next morning at six o'clock the flight left from the Sydney airport and it was scheduled to stop in Brisbane for an hour to refuel. After the short stop they took off on the long flight to Darwin. The plane was old and slow, and Gordy didn't have any idea the flight was going to be so long. Many times during the long hours, Gordy's mind would start thinking about what he would do if Kellie were still in Rabaul. After all, he hardly knew her. For all he knew, she might already be engaged to some nice young doctor.

Gordy could see her face in his mind and he sure had to admit she was cute as a bug's ear. He would sure be greatly relieved if she had been evacuated with the other nurses. The plane droned on and on; it was nighttime now, so he turned out his little light and tried to get some sleep. When they landed in Darwin early the next day, Gordy didn't think his body would ever straighten out again. The weather was already sweltering hot, and it was only eight o'clock in the morning. Gordy took a taxi from the airport into the town. He told the taxi driver to drop him off at the first hotel he came to. Gordy got himself a room with a shower. After standing under the cold shower for fifteen minutes, he crawled into bed. He was almost sleeping standing up by now. The long flight in the cramped airplane seat left him completely exhausted.

The next day at noon he awoke and felt like a million dollars. Now he was as hungry as a bull-moose. So he had another cold shower and then he went out for a meal. He had a huge steak and some eggs for starters, and for afters he had half a pie. Then Gordy walked around the town for two and a half hours. He didn't want to sit again until he had given his legs a good stretch. Sitting for eight hours, all crunched in a standard- size airplane seat was hard on an ordinary-size person. For someone Gordy's size, it was torture.

It was another scorching day in Darwin. Gordy finally went into a pub for a cold one and he saw that the pub was filled with soldiers. He bought one of the soldiers a beer and he gave Gordy the phone number of the army base. There was far too much noise in the pub, so he went back to the hotel lobby to use the phone. It took a good ten minutes to get through to the base, and when he asked for Captain Denny, he was told that the captain wouldn't be on duty till three that afternoon.

Gordy walked around the town for another three hours. When he phoned the army base again at four-thirty, the person on the other end of the line asked Gordy what he wanted with Captain Denny. Gordy had to think fast, and he said that he was a relative of Captain Denny's from Canada. Then the operator said, "Captain Denny is very busy right now, would you please leave your name and state your business?"

Gordy was stumped again for a minute, then he said, "My name is Gordon Cameron, and Captain Denny has inherited a large piece of prop- erty in Alberta, Canada. I have some papers he will have to sign in order to sell the property. Could you please tell the captain that I will be at the camp at seven o'clock?" Gordy figured they wouldn't dare not tell the captain about an inheritance he had coming in.

Gordy went into the hotel dining room and had a huge dinner. He didn't know that this would be the last good meal he would have for some time. At six-thirty Gordy took a taxi out to the army camp. It was a lot farther away than he thought it would be, or else the taxi driver took a round about way of getting there. The guard at the gate was persistent and wanted to know why he wanted to see the captain. Gordy decided he would tell the guard the same story he had told that afternoon on the phone. He was sure it would have been written down for the gate guard to check on. Gordy said, "I'm relative of Captain Denny from Canada. I have come a long way to see him about a large piece of property that he has inherited just north of Calgary, Alberta." The guard took a good look at Gordy, then he asked him for a passport or some other picture identification.

Gordy handed him his Canadian passport. He took it over to the light in the little gatehouse. Then he brought it back to Gordy and held the picture at arms length, glancing from the picture to Gordy then back to the photo. The gate guard told Gordy to stand over near the light, then he went into the hut to use the phone. Two minutes later he came out and said, "The captain will be here in a few minutes." Gordy realized the guard wanted him to stand where he could watch him and use the phone at the same time. *What a suspicious son of a sea-cook*, thought Gordy.

About four minutes later an army jeep came roaring up to the gate. The driver got out and came over to where Gordy was and said, "I'm Captain Denny, but I don't recall having any relatives in Canada."

Gordy turned around so the guard couldn't hear him and he said very quietly, "I had to tell that to the gate guard, or I don't think he would have sent for you. I really don't think that character would trust his own mother."

Gordy said, "A soldier I talked to in Sydney, a Sergeant Heck, said if anyone can help me it would be you. He thinks very highly of you, sir. My name is Gordon Cameron, and I'm a Canadian sailor. My ship was in Rabaul three months ago and I was injured while we were loading cargo. I woke up the next day in the Rabaul Hospital, and there was a cute little nurse working there by the name of Sister Gail. We became very good friends in the month I was there. I have to find out if she was evacuated with the rest of the white population or if she is still in Rabaul.

"No one with any authority will tell me a thing, and all I have to know is if she is still at the hospital or not. If she is still in Rabaul, I will have to go back and help to get her out. Don't ask me how I plan to do such a thing; I really don't know. That's why I need your help, to find out if I have to go back to Rabaul or not. I would hate like hell to go back and find out she is not there. Every time I tried to find out about her in Sydney, they told me it was classified information. I can't figure out what would be the harm of letting friend know where a certain nurse is working."

The captain looked at the big fellow for a few minutes and he thought, *This young bloke looks like he means what he says and says what he means.*

"Come with me, Canada, and we will see what we can do."

Just as Gordy stepped inside the gate, the guard said, "Hold it there, where the devil do you think your going?"

Captain Denny said, "He's going with me, Corporal."

The guard said, "Not unless you ruddy will sign for him, sir." The captain signed the register, and mumbled under his breath about overbearing pipsqueaks in uniforms.

With the captain driving like he was trying to outrun the bailiff, they drove to a large building at the far end of the army base. They went into the big gray building and walked down a long hall till they came to an office with the captain's name on the door. They went into the office and the captain got on the phone right away. After four phone calls he looked at Gordy very seriously and said, "I'm afraid I have some bad news for you, Canada. Your young lady friend is still in Rabaul. The people I talked to said that Sister Gail volunteered to stay behind to help the native girls who are still in training. The rest of the white nurses were evacuated two weeks ago."

Gordy looked down and quietly mumbled a few unsavory words he had learned in the logging camps when things were getting snagged up. Then he looked at the captain and said, "I'll have to go back and try to get her out. How I'll get there I really don't have a clue, and how I'll get her back is even a bigger question."

Captain Denny said, "You may not know this, Canada, but the Japanese are expected to be in Rabaul in the next two or three days! I'm not supposed to say anything to anybody about it, but I think you should know if you're planning on going back. It will not be a very good place for a white sheila, I'll tell you that. If you can get her out you will be doing her a ruddy great favor, mate, but I don't think I would want to be in your boots. One report I read only last night claimed the Japanese killed most of the whites in Borneo and Java when they got there. I don't see why they wouldn't do the same in Rabaul. They feel that they must show the natives of the region that the cursed whites are not invincible, after all."

The captain thought for a minute then said, "If you had enough money handy, I think I know where you could buy a boat that might just get you there. There's only one problem. It would take you three weeks to sail that distance. And I'm afraid, Canada, that would make you way too late. You could easily get off course and might never get there; it's one hell of a long distance, old cock. I don't know any local pilots that would even think of flying you to Rabaul right now, it's a bit of a sticky-wicket, mate."

Gordy said, "Maybe some pilot would be willing to fly over the place and I could parachute down?"

The captain snapped his fingers, then made another phone call. He talked to someone at a hangar and he told the person, "You tell Allan to bloody well stay put for five more minutes." Then he hung up the phone again. The captain had a big grin on his face as he said, "Come with me, Canada; maybe you will be on your way to Rabaul in no time flat!"

They ran out of the building and climbed into the jeep again, and away they went like the devil was right behind them. The large gray army buildings were soon left behind. In a matter of minutes the jeep was tearing across the tarmac of an army airdrome. There were two hangars at the far end of the runway and the captain headed for them. A single-wing aircraft was warming up near one of the hangars. When they approached the plane, they could see two men standing there waiting impatiently.

The captain got out of the jeep and told Gordy to wait there for him. He went over to talk to the two men. Captain Denny looked like he was arguing with the one fellow, but then he shook hands with the man. Then the captain came back to the jeep for Gordy. He said, "The pilot is an old cobber of mine and he has agreed to take you to Rabaul. Remember once you get into the air, there will be no turning back! My old cobber claims he could get shot for doing this, but he has to take a spotter to Rabaul anyhow and I convinced him one more passenger won't make any difference. My friend will stop on the ground just long enough to drop off the spotter and his supplies, then he will take off. Goodbye and good luck, mate; I hope you get your sheila, fair dinkum."

Gordy pulled out his wallet and took out three twenty-pound notes and handed them to the captain. He said, "Do you think you could get some one to get my gear at the Delorain Hotel and have it sent to the Anzac Shipping Company in Sydney? Then get yourself a bottle of good Scotch and have a big drink on me. Thanks again. Sergeant Heck was right, you really are a bonzer bloke."

Gordy was introduced to the two men who had been waiting by the plane and then the captain left. He walked briskly back to the jeep and drove off. Gordy felt like his last connection with civilization had just driven off and left him with these two aliens. The pilot looked at the big bloke standing beside the spotter and thought, *This is going to be rich, a peanut and an elephant.*

As soon as the two men climbed into the plane and fastened their seat belts, the door was closed and the plane taxied out onto the runway. Ten minutes later they were at the proper altitude and were on course for Rabaul. The pilot yelled at his two passengers and asked them if they were all right. The pilot sat in a seat right in front of Gordy and he turned half around in his seat and said, "I'm Allan Cooper, mate, and this skinny little runt is Archie MacCauly. Archie is going back to Rabaul to be a spotter for the army. He worked on the copra plantations of New Britain for over twenty ruddy years, would you believe it. He retired just one year ago, then he volunteered for this job. I really think he's a bit bonkers myself, or else he chewed on too many Betel nuts while he was there. Then again, maybe the horny little toad has a few old girlfriends waiting for him and he won't tell any of his mates."

Archie grinned, "I tried that retirement stuff, and it is strictly garbage, so help me. Sitting around day after day on your duff wondering what to do could make a bloke go gaga. Some of those old retired codgers do nothing but sit in the ruddy pub, from one end of the year till the next. Not me, mate; I like being outdoors. Besides nobody knows this ruddy place like I do. Who else are they going to send up here, I ask you? Some ruddy young pongo that don't know the talk, or the people? Not bloody likely, mate; I know this patch better than anyone. These people are like my ruddy family," said Archie.

Allan looked over at Gordy, and said, "My old mate Denny told us that you're going back to get some white sheila out of Rabaul, is that right? She must be a real beaut, that is all I can say, mate. I'm glad it's not me trying to pull that stunt off. I sure hope you make it, fair dinkum mate. You know that the Japs are going to occupy these islands any day? I wouldn't wait too long to clear out if I was you, mate."

While the pilot Allan was talking, Archie was quietly sizing up the young Canadian. He came to the conclusion that the big bloke looked pretty strong and could probably carry a fair load of supplies. Archie finally said, "Tell you what I'll do, Canada, you help me get my supplies up to my look-out, and I'll help you get a boat when you plan to leave the place; how does that grab you?" Gordy told Archie that he would help him any way he could.

Allan piped up then. "It is going to be a tough day for you blokes tomorrow; I think maybe you had better grab some shut eye. Don't worry, I'll wake you just before we are going to set down." The pilot then turned around and left the two in the back of the plane with their own thoughts.

Gordy looked over and noticed that the little fellow, Archie, was already dozing off. He thought, *The lucky old character just shuts his eyes and he's asleep.* After looking out the window for ten minutes and seeing nothing by the blackness below, Gordy finally drifted off to sleep. It was a tortuous and troubled sleep. After an hour or two he woke up and wondered, *What if I can't find her? Maybe she's left Rabaul for some other part of the island. Even if I find her, she might refuse to come with me.* The more Gordy thought, the more he was afraid that he had made a big mistake. Once again his head told him that she is probably engaged to some up-and-coming young doctor. *Suppose I risk my neck getting her away from the blasted island, and then she tells me she's going to marry nice Dr. Smedly!*

Not too many girls had gotten under his skin the way this little Aussie had. She sure was a beaut, he had to admit that. They did seem to be pretty friendly before he went to Sydney, and she didn't seem to be a flighty person, he thought.

For some reason he then started to think about his dad. He had promised his dad that he wouldn't do anything stupid. Gordy wondered what his dad would say about him doing this little stunt. *It's not really the smartest thing I've ever done,* he had to admit, but somebody had to come and try to get Kellie out of this jackpot. Then he thought of what old Charley would say. He would probably say something like, "The time to help your friends, Gordon, is when they need the help the most, not when they are home safe in bed."

Gordy cupped his hands around his eyes and looked out the window again, but he could see nothing but jet blackness. *There should be one blasted light down there somewhere,* he thought. He sure hoped the darkness was not a bad omen. Gordy then looked over at the scrawny little character, Archie, snoring away as though he didn't have a worry in the world. *I sure hope the little guy meant what he said; that he would help me get a boat when I want to leave Rabaul.* He hadn't actually gave a lot of thought about how he was going to get Kellie back to Aussie. A boat would probably be the only way, he had to admit.

The plane droned on through the darkness and Gordy finally dozed off again. Once more the sleep was tortured and not too restful.

Chapter Six

Big Gordy Back

Gordy kept dozing on and off, restlessly squirming around in his seat as the hours dragged by. His whole life seemed to be flitting across his mind on a continuous film. Half an hour before the plane was to land, Allan yelled out, "Come on, mates, wake up! Snap out of it, mates, we will be going in soon." It seemed to Gordy that he had just drifted into a decent sleep and now he was being woken up.

Allan had brought a large thermos of tea and some sandwiches with him, so he shared them with Archie and Gordy. "I want to remind you blokes that there will be no time to waste when we hit the ground. When I yell, you have to open the door and start throwing the supplies out. Don't jump out then or you'll break your ruddy leg I will stop the plane just long enough for you to get on the ground, then I will be gone. I don't want to be on the ground long enough for anyone to see the plane and report it. If the plane is reported, then someone will want to know what it was doing here. It won't take a smart fly-fella long to figure it out."

Gordy was halfway through his second cup of tea and a sandwich, when his thinking went fuzzy again. He again thought, *Suppose Kellie really doesn't want to come with me, what the devil will I do? You can't make someone come with you if they really don't want to go.* Gordy chased the thought back and forth in his mind a few more times. Then he decided he would have to play it by ear when the time came. Besides he reasoned, *I am here now so I might as well have a go at getting her home. Even if I don't succeed it would be better than not doing anything.*

They could feel the plane suddenly start losing altitude. Gordy took another quick look out the window, again there were no lights. They were going down at a fairly steep angle now and losing speed fast. *Lord love a duck*, Gordy thought, *I sure hope Allan can see the ground and knows what he is doing or all my fretting is going to be for nothing!*

The plane suddenly leveled out just as Allan yelled, "Hang on!" The plane hit the tarmac real hard and then taxied to the far end of the runway. Then Allan yelled, "Right on, mates, open the door and start throwing your gear out!" When the plane turned around and came to a full stop, Archie and Gordy lowered themselves to the tarmac. The door slammed shut behind them the minute they hit the ground, and the little plane started roaring down the runway almost immediately. As Allan had not put his landing lights on, within a minute the plane had vanished into the darkness.

All of the six crates were about the same size. Archie picked up two of them and walked away. There were four more crates, so Gordy picked them all up and took off after Archie. *The young fellow won't go far with that load,* thought Archie. For two full hours they never stopped or slowed down, then Archie said, "Let's stop for a cuppa tea mate; we have made a ruddy good start." Archie dug into one of the crates and pulled out a small stove and a billycan for the tea. They had their tea and some hardtack biscuits spread with vegimite. It certainly was not what Gordy considered a meal by any stretch of the imagination, but it was better than nothing.

After their cuppa tea, Archie packed up the little stove and the billy. Then they picked up the crates and took off up the faint trail again. At about four that afternoon they stopped once more. The stove came out and the billycan was put on for the tea once more. Of course biscuits and vegimite were spread for eating again. Archie seemed to thrive on the blasted things.

While they were slowly drinking their second cup of strong tea, they faintly heard the sound of planes. The planes flew high and very fast but they both knew they were Japanese Zeros. Five minutes later they returned, flying lower and a lot slower. Twice more the Japanese planes flew slowly over the area; each time they would change directions and looked the whole place over.

Archie looked over at Gordy for a minute, then said, "Well mate, that little air show we just watched means only one ruddy thing. The Nips will be here tomorrow! I don't think we have much time to spare, Canada, if we are going to get your sheila. I'll lay odds that their ruddy navy will sail right into the harbor tomorrow. They know there is nobody here to take a shot at them now. I think we had better go into Rabaul tonight and get that little sheila of yours, fair dinkum. Let's park everything here and we'll pick it up after we get your friend. No one will touch the stuff I'm sure."

They finished their tea and put everything away. Then they took off down the same path that they had just come up. As they had no heavy crates to carry they made much better time, arriving at the edge of the airport just as it was getting dark. The small airport buildings looked completely deserted. There was not one light to be seen and not a soul anywhere; the whole place had been completely abandoned.

Archie told Gordy, "You wait here, Canada, there should be an old truck over by that far hangar, and if it still works, we will borrow it for awhile." Archie then disappeared into the darkness. Gordy was left standing in the gloom, he started thinking about those Japanese planes that had flown over the town earlier. He hoped that the planes would convince Kellie to come with him without too much fuss. Gordy realized he would have been too late to be of any help to Kellie if he had not arrived when he did. Then he thought, *Where the devil is Archie? If that little squirt takes off on me, I'll have a hard time finding the hospital in the dead of night, let alone rescue anyone.*

It was a good half an hour later before Gordy heard the sound of a motor; it did not sound too healthy but it was coming closer, he did know that. He could make out a pair of very dim headlights, which were also coming his way. Finally an old battered pickup truck stopped beside Gordy. "You call for a cab, mate?" said Archie.

The old truck had no model number or make stamped on it, and looked like it had been made in someone's backyard. "Old Suzy still goes!" Archie said. "Would you believe, I sold the airport this old bucket of rust for fifty quid when I retired? It used to have eight cylinders going at the same time when I sold it. Now only about four of them are working but it still moves, and that's all that counts right now."

There were no doors on Old Suzy so it wasn't hard getting in, but staying in proved to be a bit of a problem. Gordy climbed into the cab of the dilapidated old truck and hoped he didn't sit on a snake or poisonous spider or something else just as dangerous. He had heard a lot of stories about how reptiles and spiders just loved making nests in old pieces of machinery.

Archie let out the clutch and the old crate jumped ahead about three feet. "I'll be blowed," said Archie, "they still haven't fixed the first gear in Old Suzy!" Archie seemed to hit every pothole in the road on the ten-mile drive to town; it was almost like he was trying to hit them. Gordy was nearly thrown out of the cab two or three different times. Archie claimed Old Suzy had nearly a million miles on the odometer.

They eventually reached the edge of town and Archie stopped the old truck on the side of the road. He turned off the motor and said, "I think we had better leave Old Suzy here, or the whole town will know we have arrived." They started walking the four city blocks to the hospital. When they had walked about three blocks, Archie asked, "Got any idea what you're going to do, Canada, if your friend won't come with you? You know, some of these sheilas can be pretty funny at times."

"Well I have been giving that a lot of thought, Archie; I figure I'll have to just pick her up and take her. It won't be too pleasant around here for a white girl if she stays. Even if I don't manage to get her back home alive, I don't think it would be as bad as staying here," said Gordy.

The streets of the town were deserted; not even a dog was on the street. Everyone on the whole island had seen those Japanese planes earlier in the day, then headed for the hills. They could make out the dark outline of the hospital from a good block away. There were no lights showing, but you could still make it out. When they got to the hospital, Archie said, "I think it best if we go up the back way. We don't want the whole blooming staff knowing we are here." They quietly went up the wooden stairs at the back of the hospital and found a heavy door with a thick glass window barring their way. Naturally, it was locked from the inside.

Gordy said, "How do you figure on getting into the hospital, old timer?" Archie replied, "We will have to wait here till one of the girls makes her rounds, then we will simply knock on the ruddy door." They waited and waited but still no one appeared to be moving inside. Archie tried to see the time on his watch, but it was far too dark. "They should be coming soon mate. If someone doesn't come in the next half hour I'll have to go around to the front door."

A good twenty minutes went by before they saw the movement of someone through the glass window, going from room to room on her rounds. When the girl got near the thick back door, Archie rapped on the window half a dozen times. The frightened little native girl nearly jumped out of her skin. She opened the door slowly and asked who they were, and what they wanted. Archie spoke quietly in his best pidgin English, "Me Archie fella, and this big fella Gordy. We come to get Sister Gail. Yella fellas come tomorrow and kill all white fellas. Gordy fella, come take Sister Gail away tonight. Can you take us to Sister Gail, please?" The little native girl remembered Gordy fella, and she knew Sister Kellie liked him a lot.

The little native girl nodded her head and said, "Yes, I take you to Sister Kellie, she very 'fraid. When plane fly over she very very 'fraid, she be much glad to see big Gordy fella." The girl told them to be very quiet so as not to wake anyone. They went down a long hallway and stopped in front of a door. The girl tapped lightly on the door. "Yes, what is it you want?" a voice asked. "Big Gordy back, big Gordy back!" announced the native girl.

There was no further reply, but there was some moving around in the room. The little native girl tapped on the door again. She said, "Sister Kellie, are you all right? Big Gordy fella come for you, take you away tonight." There was no more talking from inside the room but there was more shuffling around. The latch in the door clicked and the door finally opened. Kellie took one look at Gordy and fainted. He gently picked her up and put her on the bed. Two minutes later Kellie sat bolt upright and said, "I'll be blowed, what are you doing here Gordon? Where did you come from, and why are you ruddy well here? Are you stark raving mad? Don't you know that the Japanese will be here any day now? You had better get out of here as fast as you can, are you stark raving mad?" Kellie was talking so fast she was tripping over her words. She stopped for a minute then started all over again. "What are you doing here? Don't you know what's going to happen to you if the Japanese catch you, are you off your ruddy trolley altogether?"

Gordy put up his large hand as a signal for her to stop ranting and raving. "That is exactly why I am here, little one. The Japanese won't hurt the natives because they need them. But the whites are their enemy and will be killed; you can count on that. The Japs have to show the natives in the area that they are going to run things from now on. So grab a few things and stick them into a small bag and let's get the devil out of here. We have already done enough palavering, little one!"

Kellie looked square at Gordy and said, "I really can't go; I have never broken my word and I'm not going to start now. I volunteered to stay and help the native girls who have been in training for the last four years. Besides, I don't think the Japanese will hurt anyone in the medical field. They need doctors and nurses just as much as white people do," she insisted.

Archie spoke up then and said, "Listen love, if you don't come with us now you will be ruddy well dead by this time next week, or you will wish you were. I don't know if this big bloke can get you home, but he will have a ruddy good go at it!"

Kellie asked them to wait in the hall while she changed, and when they went out of the room she locked the door. After a few minutes, Archie said to Gordy, "Tell your friend not to put any white things on, they would be too easy to spot."

Gordy went to the door and said, "Kellie, Archie said he didn't think it wise to put any white things on."

Kellie answered, "I'm not going with you, Gordy, I told them I would stay here."

Gordy grabbed the door handle and pulled the door right out of the door jam, then he propped the door in the hallway. He picked Kellie up like a side of beef and threw her over his shoulder. As he went out the door he said to Archie, "Get the little girl to give you a hand to stick some things in a bag, I'll wait for you at the truck."

The little native girl thought this Gordy fella is one smart white man, this is the way the men of the islands have been getting their women for years. She had a big smile on her face. *Wait till the other nurses hear about this*, she thought.

Kellie was sobbing and at the same time threatening Gordy with all kinds of wild and scary things if he did not put her down right away. She wanted to say that she would bash him up but she knew that sounded to ridiculous under the circumstances. This had been one bad day: First the Japanese planes scared the pants off everyone, now this.

When she had quieted down a bit she wondered why on earth he would risk his life to come back just for her. *The big bozo hardly knows me,* she thought. *Why would he come back? The dumbest thing I ever did in my whole life was to stay behind when the others left. What a ruddy dodo I was!* she thought.

Then it dawned on her that Gordy was here to help and nobody else came, so stop complaining. He might must take her at her word and drop her right here. Gordy strode along at a normal walking speed like she weighed absolutely nothing. Kellie thought, *If this big bozo thinks he's going to push me around he's got another thing coming. He may be big as a ruddy house but he's not going to browbeat me. I'll give him a swift kick where it hurts the most if he gets too frisky with me.* Then she thought back to the time she rode with him in the ambulance and how he kissed her twice. She liked that. He also wrote her letters from Sydney; they too were nice warm serious letters. Then she thought, *The big gorilla probably writes nice warm letters to half a dozen girls around the world.*

When they finally reached the place where the truck was parked, Gordy set Kellie down on the ground. He held onto her though; he didn't relish the thought of chasing an irate nurse all over town in the middle of the night. "Now listen to me, little one, I don't know if I can get you home or not," he said softly. "I know it is better to die fighting than to just sit on your duff, waiting to be led to the slaughter. When it comes time to leave the island and you want to stay here, I won't object. I promise."

Kellie wondered, *What exactly did he mean by that remark? Does he want to help me get home or doesn't he?* Kellie asked him, "Tell me Gordon, what made you come back here anyway? And don't tell me you just happened to be in the neighborhood. I really don't know about you, Gordon Cameron; sometimes you really have me confused."

Archie arrived at the truck just at that moment and said, "Let's get out of here, mate, we have to be a long way from here by sunup." Gordy stuck Kellie into the cab and got in after her. Then Archie climbed in on the other side and started up the old jalopy. He put the old bucket of bolts into gear and again it made a great leap forward. Gordy almost fell out when it lurched forward, but when Old Suzy finally got going, all went well.

Archie tried his best to miss the potholes in the road, but there were just too many of them. After being bounced around the cab for ten minutes, Kellie thought, *If this is their idea of a great escape plan, I'm in a lot of trouble.*

The old crate bumped and jarred its way back to the airport. When they finally got there, Archie stopped and let them off by the trail. He told them, "Wait here; I want to get this old buggy back in the exact same place it was in before I borrowed it. I don't want anyone to even suspect it was used."

Archie took off into the blackness of the night, leaving Gordy and Kellie all alone for the first time. It was a little tense for the first few minutes. Gordy had an idea that Kellie might think his motives for coming back for her were not quite that noble. Kellie then said, "Why don't you tell me, Gordon, why did you come back, you barely know me? How do I know you're not already married to half a dozen girls?"

Gordy was stumped for a minute, then said, "I had to come back; I really had no choice. You see, I have this old aunt in Vancouver and she reads people's tea leaves, believe it or not. It is absolutely uncanny the things my old aunt can see in tea leaves. One day she read my tea leaves and she told me I was going to be injured on a ship in a faraway port. This old aunt of mine then said the first woman I see when I wake up would be the woman I would spend the rest of my life with. So you see, little one, I had to come back. I had no choice, it was written in the tea leaves." Gordy didn't say any more for a minute, then he said, "I'll tell you, Kellie, my dear old aunt is hardly ever wrong. As a matter of fact, I've never heard of her making a single mistake, so help me."

Kellie thought this was either the biggest pile of malarkey she had ever heard in her whole life or the most amazing story in the world. She was trying as hard she could to think of something to say, but nothing would come to mind. All she could think was, *This is ruddy bizarre to say the least. An old aunt who reads people's tea leaves. This big bozo expects me to believe a story like that; he must think I'm a bit bonkers.*

Then Gordy added, "This dear old aunt of mine claims everything is written down when we are born. She also claims and believes fervently that there is a plan for everyone. I know it sounds strange, but as I've said, my dear old aunt is rarely every wrong."

Just then, Archie turned up and Kellie had no chance to ask any more questions. Archie said, "Let's get the show on the road, mate. We have to move a long way from here before daylight." He took off up the trail and, although Gordy and Kellie tried to keep up with him, Archie was soon out of sight. He was a small wiry man and he could make his short legs move at an amazing speed. Gordy called to him and asked him if he could to slow it down a bit, when they couldn't see him anymore. Archie came back to where they were and he promised to put the brake on a bit. Gordy then took the small bag from Kellie. He held her small hand in his big paw and away they went once more. They walked continuously for over four hours, and they were bushed, especially Kellie. She had put in a good twelve-hour shift at work before Gordy had showed up to rescue her.

They finally reached the place where they had left the crates. They were still there and had not been moved or disturbed in any way. Archie dug out the little stove and put the billy on for a cup of strong tea. They all needed a cuppa in the worst way. Poor Kellie looked like she was going to drop on the spot. Archie spread some more crackers with vegimite, to sustain them till they could cook a meal.

The sky was just starting to get light and they were pooped, so Archie suggested they rest where they were for a couple hours. Kellie was sound asleep in a matter of minutes. She was sitting curled up on the ground and leaning against the trunk of a palm tree. Gordy looked at her and thought about how small she was. Archie and Gordy also propped themselves against a tree and dozed off in no time flat.

Three and a half hours later they woke with a start, as the sudden roar of aircraft overhead almost deafened them. A flight of large Japanese transport planes were coming in for a landing at the airport. The planes didn't circle around or hesitate one bit; they made a direct approach to the runway. Apparently they had been assured they would have no enemy to bother with. The war was spreading faster than anyone predicted.

Archie lit the little stove again and made another cup of tea. They each had two biscuits with vegimite spread on them for breakfast. They ate fast as they could and were eager to get as far from the airport as was possible. While they were busy sticking everything back into their respective crates, Kellie suddenly grabbed Gordy's arm. He looked at her and wondered what was wrong now. He saw that she was staring at something on the trail that they had came up. It took nearly a minute before Gordy saw anything. When he did, he turned to Archie and said, "Hold it a minute, old timer, I think we have some company. Have you any suggestions what would be the best way to handle these fellows?"

Archie looked up and saw the two natives standing perfectly still and watching them. Archie laughed and said, "Don't be nervous, mate, these people gave up head hunting years ago. The natives around here are some of the best and friendliest people I've ever worked with, fair dinkum."

The two men had beautiful physiques, and when they stood perfectly still, they blended into the background. At first they looked just like two ebony statues. Archie smiled and walked over to the two men, greeting them like old members of the family. He began speaking to them in their own dialect. *They all seemed to be talking at the same time,* thought Gordy. They laughed a couple of times and looked over at Gordy and Kellie. Then the two men came back with Archie to where Kellie and Gordy were standing, who were not too sure what to do or how to act. Archie had a big smile on his wrinkled old face, and said, "These are very old friends of mine; I have known both men and their families for many years.

"This fellow here is George. He was my number-one man for a long long time. And this fella is Dan, him George fellow's older brother. Dan fella also worked for me for a long long time. They have agreed to help us move the crates to that ridge up ahead." The two natives had big smiles on their strong friendly faces, showing off their beautiful white teeth. They were not as tall as Gordy, but both were wonderful-looking specimens of manhood. Archie had told them how Gordy walked into the big hospital, and how he threw nurse Kellie over his shoulder, just like the native fellas do. Then he walked right out of the hospital with her. They thought Gordy must be one smart white man. Most other white men they had seen weren't smart enough to do that. In their minds, throwing the woman you love over your shoulder and taking her home is the only way to make sure you get the right woman.

George fella and his brother Dan helped move the crates about fifteen miles up the path. From this ridge, Archie claimed he would have a clear view of the ships coming into the harbor and also the airport. It took them nearly five hours to reach the spot that Archie had chosen for a hut. It wasn't nearly so strenuous and tiring with the extra help. George fella and Dan promised to come back the next morning to put up the hut Archie would need for his spotting job. Then the two men left to go back to their own village. Archie explained to Gordy and Kellie how the brothers had started working for him when they were just kids.

Archie dug out the little stove once more and the billy was put on for tea. He also opened one can of bully beef and split it between the three of them. This was supposed to be their supper. Gordy didn't think too highly of Archie's food supply. Anyway, the day was finished and poor Kellie was asleep on her feet, so Archie dug out a foldaway cot and a couple of old army blankets. He suggested that Kellie use the cot to get some shut eye. Then he gave Gordy a sleeping bag, which was in another crate. It too looked like old army issue, from some war someplace. That left only an old piece of canvas for Archie, but he didn't seem to mind at all; he claimed he could sleep on a bed of nails.

Gordy crawled into the old army sleeping bag. He suddenly realized that he had got Kellie away from the hospital just in the nick of time. Now he had to find a way to get her back to Australia. He was chasing that problem over and over in his mind when he drifted off into a deep sleep. The next morning, planes started to arrive at the airport. Then many other different types of planes started coming in. They could see the Zeros circling around at a much higher altitude, covering the landing. Archie said, "It wouldn't surprise me if the harbor wouldn't be filled with battleships by noon. I think maybe I had better get my radio into operation pretty quick." Archie looked over at Gordy. "I'll tell you one thing, mate, we just got your young lady out in the nick, fair dinkum." Kellie was very quiet; she was thinking about the native girls at the hospital. She knew they would be very scared right now.

Archie started up the little stove and put the billy on to make some tea, and of course they had some more of the hardtack biscuits. Gordy didn't quite know how to tell Archie that he was getting a little tired of biscuits for breakfast, lunch, and dinner. It was almost at the point where he needed some real honest-to-God meat, or at least something that tasted like meat. The bully-beef was all right, but he could have quite easily eaten three cans of the stuff himself. There wasn't enough in one can to even take the wrinkles out of his stomach. In a nonchalant way, Gordy said, "Tell me something Archie, are there any wild animals on this island? I feel a great hunger for some meat of some kind, tea and biscuits don't do much for me really. The native people must eat meat of some kind, sometime."

With a grin on his face, Archie said, "There are some wild pigs in the bush, but they are so fast that you can never get a shot at them. The natives catch the odd one in a trap, but even they have trouble with the blighters. But I have to admit, mate, they make a tasty meal, and there is an old rifle in that crate over there if you want to have a go."

Gordy went over and undid the crate Archie had indicated. He took out an old World War I army rifle, and after he made sure every part worked as it should, he looked through the barrel. Archie watched him as he took only two shells out of the box. Gordy put one shell in the chamber and on in his shirt pocket. Archie though, *Is he trying to show off in front of Kellie? The young bucks are all the same no matter where they come from.*

Just at that moment, George fella and Dan showed up. Dan fella had brought his twelve-year-old son with him. Dan fella explained, "My son BoBo says he wants to help build hut so I bring him, he good number-one son."

Archie thanked them for coming and told them he would give them a can of tobacco each for helping him. He said he remembered BoBo when he was just a little monkey."

Archie then said, "Gordy fella wants to go hunt for pig in the bush. I don't suppose BoBo knows where the pigs live in the bush? Maybe he can lead Gordy fella to pigs' home!" BoBo jumped up and down with excitement and claimed he knew where all pigs lived, and he could be number-one guide for Gordy fella.

Dan said, "Maybe Gordy fella don't need guide, hunt better alone." Gordy laughed and said, "Only a poor hunter would turn down a guide who knows where all the pigs live. A old friend of mine used to say good guides are like good intentions—no good unless they are used."

They all sat around and talked for some time. Archie made some tea and told the two brothers what he knew about the planes that flew over. He then said, "I don't think the Japanese will hurt the native people, but I'm not sure. Some of the yellow fellas are real bad people. I'd advise George fella and Dan move their families up into the mountains till the yellow fellows go away." He knew that idea could prove to be hazardous to their health also, because the mountain people were still very primitive and liked the odd war. Archie thought he had better keep his advice to himself and let them work out their own problems. BoBo was getting impatient; he wanted to go hunting, not sit around and talking all day.

Kellie said, "I used to go hunting rabbits with my dad when I was young, so I want to go hunting too." Gordy thought she would be out of place watching George and Dan putting up a hut, so he said she would be welcome. BoBo didn't seem overly excited about a female coming on his hunting trip. After all, it was men's work to supply the meat.

The three of them took off into the bush, BoBo in the front doing the guiding and Kellie in the rear. Gordy hoped he hasn't shot his big mouth off in the wrong place. He did know how to hunt as well as any man, he knew that. He desperately needed some solid food; he felt like he was going to starve to death living on tea and crackers. Gordy felt if he didn't get some meat to eat real soon, Kellie might have to rescue *him*.

Chapter Seven

The Hut

In the twenty-four years he had worked on the island, Archie had seen the islanders put up their huts hundreds of times. But it still amazed him how they could do it so fast and not have the things fall down with the first strong wind. He knew they started learning the skill of hut-making when they were little lads, and the older men let them do the part of the job they liked doing the best. The system worked out well; each boy seemed to enjoy doing a certain job so they specialized in that part of the operation. George fella and Dan threw up the frame in no time flat; then they both gathered up a large pile of foliage. George started throwing the foliage up to Dan, who put it in place and tied it all in one motion. His hands moved so fast, you couldn't really see the knot being made, but each set of leaves was separately tied and they stayed tied.

Two and a half hours later the hut was up, all finished. It was not a large hut because that would be too easy to spot from the air. The main idea was to keep the hut a secret from the Japanese as long as possible. Archie gave them each a can of tobacco and then made a cup of tea for his two friends. They sat around admiring their work, drinking tea and smoking.

BoBo, Kellie, and Gordy had started to get into a damp marshy area where the flies came in clouds so thick as times that they could hardly see BoBo. Suddenly the earth shook violently and knocked Gordy right off of his feet. He looked at Kellie, and exclaimed, "What the hell was that?"

Kellie saw the look on Gordy's face, she then said, "That was only a small earthquake, there will be a few smaller ones in a minute or two. After a while you get sort of used to them." BoBo thought it was real funny that

46

a big fella like Gordy should be so startled with a little quake. He had grown up with the earth shaking every other week. Sometimes a volcano would erupt at the same time just to add to the fun.

Kellie told Gordy that when she first came to work at Rabaul she nearly had a nervous breakdown. Every few days the earth would shake like jelly; she almost quit her job two or three times. She gradually got used to the excitement and now they didn't even faze her. After another ten minutes of walking, BoBo came to a halt and pointed to a large area of low bushes. Gordy could hear the grunting of pigs; he patted BoBo on his fuzzy head and signaled for him to get behind him. Gordy crouched down and rested his elbow on his knee; he clicked the safety catch off. Then he listened intently for a good five minutes. Kellie wondered what in the world he was waiting for. *He knows there are pigs in the bush; why doesn't he go in and get one?*

Gordy waited till there was no noise in the bush, then he made a grunt like a pig. There was suddenly more grunting in the bush. Gordy waited for another few minutes, then he grunted again. The bush suddenly parted, and there was a fair-sized pig standing there looking at him, The pig grunted again, and Gordy shot him before he finished the grunt. The porker was dead before it hit the ground.

Gordy handed the rifle to BoBo, who was standing right behind him. Then he took out the small knife that was always on his belt. With one swift cut he slit the belly of the pig open. Gordy made a few more quick cuts, then he dumped the innards on the ground. After wiping the blade of the knife off, he slid it back in its sheath. Then Gordy grabbed the pig's two front legs in one hand and sauntered off, dragging the pig behind him. It had all happened in a few very fast movements. BoBo and Kellie found themselves standing there with their mouths hanging open in disbelief.

By the time the two of them snapped out of their trance, Gordy was nearly out of sight, and they both had to run to catch up to him. Finally they caught up and BoBo ran on ahead. BoBo got to the hut and the other men first, where he started chattering away in his own dialect to his dad and George fella. They had faintly heard the one shot and naturally figured that it had not found the target. So it surprised them when Gordy came into the clearing, dragging the fairly large pig.

Kellie was trying to keep up to Gordy, and the sight of the big bloke dragging the pig as though it had no weight at all caused her to think, *Maybe this character might get me home after all.* The way he had cut the pig open and had taken out the insides, made her a bit queasy for a minute, but it had also astounded her.

When Gordy strolled into the small clearing with the pig, Archie looked at Gordy in a whole new light. Over the years he worked on the island, he had seen a lot of blokes who claimed to be the expert hunters. Most of them had a hard time shooting the lively small pigs on the island. Some of the poor pigs looked like a sieve by the time some of these so-called hunters brought them in. Dan finally said, "Gordy fella number-one hunter, teach BoBo how to shoot pig like great hunter. Dan and BoBo take pig to village, George fella, bring Gordy fella and Archie fella and Mary to village for kiki."

"Dan fella, that is a number-one good idea, the last thing we want is smoke coming from this area. The Japanese would be sure to investigate people so close to the airport. Dan fella go to village now; we put crate in hut and clean up, then we all come to village belong Dan." But an hour after Dan and BoBo had departed, they were still sitting on the crates, admiring the hut and contemplating the feed of ham they would be eating later. They were so engrossed in their talking that they never heard the small Japanese plane till it was right overhead. It was a small spotter plane and it circled the clearing slowly and then took off for the airport.

Archie banged himself on the head and said, "I'll be a cross-eyed dingo, I think we have sat on our duffs too ruddy long. The pilot of that plane will surely report what he saw, and by tomorrow you can bet there will be some army people here to investigate. Of all the stupid blasted things to do! A mentally defective sheep wouldn't be as dumb as I am sometimes. So help me, you would think I was working for the ruddy Nips."

Archie looked dejected and kept shaking his head, he didn't say a word for a few minutes. Then he seemed to make up his mind and said, "We will have to move most of these supplies right now and come back for the rest of them early tomorrow morning. There is another ridge up ahead about five miles; it is not nearly as good as this place but I think we had better move the supplies there." Archie put the radio crate in the hut because it was the heaviest. He knew everyone was getting hungry and a little edgy, so they packed up the rest of the crates as fast as they could and took off for the ridge.

When they finally reached the other ridge and had dragged all the crates up onto a small ledge, George gathered up some foliage to keep any rain off the boxes. Then they took off for George's village, which was about five miles away. By the time George and the honored guests arrived, the pig was cooked and everyone was anxious to eat. As Gordy fella had shot the pig, he had the first choice of the parts he wanted to eat. The natives thought it a little odd that he would pick one of the back legs. There were also great matted plates of cooked fruits and many things that Gordy had never seen before. The islanders of the South Seas know how to throw a party as few people do. They were masters of putting on a feast and many earlier visitors to the region wound up as the main course at some of their festivals.

Two hours later the meal was over and most of the pig had been devoured. There were just a few scraps left over and these were given to the dogs. It was now time for the entertainment. It was suggested that the hunter must get up and tell the rest of the diners how he tracked the prey and finally shot it. Gordy thought this would be part of their tradition. Nearly all people who hunt as a way of life love to revel in the exploits of the hunter involved.

His old Indian friend, Charley, had told him many times that the taste of the meat will soon be forgotten, but the telling of the hunt will last a life-time. Charley also used to say that even the poorest hunter will live on in legend if he learns to tell a mighty story. And so the storyteller rose to spread out the second course of the feast. He took his time looking over the vil-lagers carefully, choosing the exact right time to start. He closed his eyes for a minute and pictured over in his mind the exact moment the hunt started and ended.

In a loud voice that could be heard by all, Gordy said, "It was the great guide I had today which made the hunt a success." He described in detail how he followed BoBo through the bush, to the exact place where the pigs lived. He told them about being knocked down by the earthquake and he wobbled his knees to show how they shook. Then he showed them, with a great flair, how he crouched down and took careful aim. He put his hand up to his ear to show how he listened to the pigs talking. It was only after he had listened to the pigs talking that he talked to them. Gordy then made a grunt like a pig. He told them that one of the pigs came out of the bushes to investigate the new pig in the neighborhood; the one who was making the strange grunts.

When the pig came out of the bush he grunted at Gordy, and that was his last grunt. Gordy pretended to fire the rifle, then he rolled over as if he were dead. The twenty-odd people all clapped like mad. The meal had been good but the entertainment was even better. BoBo was so happy, his dad thought he would bust. He had never seen the lad so excited. The party went on for an hour or so, then Gordy, Archie, and Kellie headed back to their camp. After their first real good meal in days they all felt much better, but the fatigue of the last few days had finally caught up with them. When they arrived back at their camp, they got the cot and things out of crates and were asleep in a matter of minutes. It was the first time Gordy had gone to sleep with a full stomach since he left Darwin, and it put him into a deep contented sleep. Archie never did eat large meals, so it more than satisfied his scrawny stomach.

Kellie, for the first time in a month, went to sleep feeling like she just might see good old Aussie once more. Seeing Gordy killing the pig and doing all those things so easily made her feel a little safer. They all slept so soundly that night; even the patrol plane didn't waken them the next morning.

Archie got up first and was sitting on one of the crates when Gordy stirred. "Don't move, mate," said Archie. "I think that there are some army people down at that hut; it looks like Jap soldiers from here. They have some-one down on the ground, and I have a stinking feeling it's George or Dan."

Very slowly Archie opened up one of the crates and got out the binoculars. When he gradually brought them up to look through, he couldn't believe his eyes. "I was right, they have George down on the ground and he's not moving!"

Archie passed the binoculars to Gordy, who stared through them for about three or four minutes before he said anything. Then he said, "I think your friend George is all right; there are two soldiers guarding him and I don't think they guard dead people. Archie, if you want, I'll take the rifle down there and try to help your friend. I'm a good shot, but if you would rather go that will be all right with me." Archie agreed that he was a little too old for these kinds of heroics. "Don't come down there, Archie, no matter what happens to me. Take care of Kellie, and don't move and inch till I get back." Gordy loaded a full clip into the rifle this time, and like an eel, he slowly slid along the rocky volcanic surface that led down from the ledge.

Kellie was awake by this time. She knew that something was wrong right away and she asked Archie what was happening. Gordy had slithered his way down the rocky path by this time and finally reached the level ground. Archie told Kellie what was going on down at the hut, and that Gordy didn't want them to move. When Kellie tried to see what Gordy was doing, she couldn't actually see him moving at all. Then each time she looked he was in a different place. All of a sudden he disappeared from view. She tried as hard as she could to see him, but he had completely vanished.

Archie gently took her arm and said, "Don't worry love; I believe he will be all right. The young bloke seems to know what he's doing." Kellie started to weep. *What the heck will I do if Gordy gets captured or killed?* she thought. Archie was a tough old bloke all right, but she didn't think he would be able to get her back home. Maybe she should have stayed in the hospital after all. Dr. Alvarez kept saying the Japanese wouldn't hurt them, that they never bother the medical people. *How would he know?* Many people at the hospital had wondered. He told some of the native nurses that he had studied in Tokyo, and he knew the Japanese people well. (Dr. Alvarez was tried in a military court after the war as a Japanese spy. He was sentenced to ten years in jail.)

Gordy kept a palm-tree trunk between himself and the two soldiers at all times. He slowly inched himself along the ground till he could clearly see the two soldiers standing over poor George. One of the soldiers was a big mean-looking guy who looked like he would enjoy sticking a bayonet into George. The other soldier was smaller and he wore thick glasses. *He probably takes a lot of guff from the big guy*, thought Gordy.

There was some noise coming from inside the hut. It startled Gordy, and it also meant that there were at least three soldiers. Gordy got as close to the ground as he could, then he inched ever so slowly over to where he could still see the two soldiers outside, as well as the front of the hut.

He didn't move again or even so much as blink an eye. He had learned from his old Indian friend Charley that if you remain perfectly still, often people and animals will look right at you and not see you. Move only the slightest fraction and they see the movement, then they see you. Gordy waited till he heard the man inside smashing something, then he shot the smaller soldier in the middle of his chest. The big ape had just kicked poor George and he still didn't have his foot down on the ground when Gordy shot him in the throat. He too went over backwards. They were both stone dead before they hit the ground. He swung the barrel lightly and pointed it at the door while hugging the ground, but no one came out and there was no other movement inside.

Gordy didn't so much as blink an eye or move a muscle. He knew that the other soldier would be trying to peek through the hut's foliage to try and see where the enemy was hiding. The third soldier in the hut did not dare return to his base without his comrades. He had to somehow locate whoever had shot his friends. He also knew for certain that he too would be shot if he went out the front door of the hut. The Japanese soldier was between a rock and a hard place. He had not been in the army long, yet he knew that he had to at least try to kill his enemy.

Foremost in his mind was the knowledge that to go back to the army base and say he had not at least tried to avenge the killing of his friends would lead to a court-martial and disgrace. Maybe even an execution, just as an example to the rest of the troops of his regiment.

Gordy still didn't move or even blink an eye; he just kept the rifle barrel pointed at the door of the hut. After an hour went by, Gordy knew that the soldier was in a position where he had to try something. He couldn't stay in there till the war ended. Gordy also figured the Japanese soldier would have to come out of the other side of the hut so he could sneak up on him. Ever so slowly Gordy started to inch himself backward, keeping the rifle always pointed at the hut. Time was slipping by and Gordy knew that the soldier had to make a move soon.

Gordy edged himself about ten feet backwards, then he stopped and waited. Nearly two hours went by before he saw the slightest movement out of the corner of his eye. Another ten minutes went by. Then he saw another slight movement. Gordy wanted to turn his head in the worst way, just to see what the soldier was doing. He knew the other man was making a fatal error and would soon join his two friends. Gordy never so much as twitched a muscle and soon the Japanese soldier crawled another foot forward. Then he slowly raised his head to look up into the treetops. He saw his friends fall backwards, so he thought they had been shot by someone in a tree. The Japanese soldiers had been trained to get into a treetop and wait for the enemy to appear. Then they could pick them off one by one from a distance.

The young soldier's heart was pounding like a trip-hammer and his nerves were stretched to the extreme, but there was no going back. Like a snail, he slowly crawled forward one more time. Then he raised his head right into the line with Gordy's sights. When Gordy slowly squeezed the trigger, the soldier never even heard the shot. He joined his two friends in heaven without ever having seen his enemy.

Gordy saw George slowly sit up and hold his fuzzy head in his hands, so he knew that it was all clear. If there had been more than three Japanese soldiers at the camp, George would have remained where he was. Gordy looked all around very carefully, in case George had been knocked out before more soldiers had shown up. Nothing seemed to be moving anywhere, so he got up very slowly. As he approached the third soldier, Gordy saw that the far side of his head was missing and felt very sorry for him. Gordy knew it was a case of him or me, so he held no bad feeling toward the soldier. He grabbed the dead soldier by the belt, then he dragged him over to the edge of a small ravine and dropped him over.

Gordy then went over to George and asked him if he was all right. George had a headache that would stop a water buffalo dead in its tracks, but other than that he was not hurt. Gordy said, "George, you get that little yella fella and follow me; we will throw him in the hole. I think we should leave here real fast, maybe more yella fellas will come." After Gordy had looked at the radio and found it smashed up, they took off to where Archie and Kellie were waiting to hear what had happened.

When the two men got back to the ledge, Kellie jumped up and gave Gordy a big hug. Kellie said, "We heard the shots but we had no idea who had shot who. Why do you have to keep scaring people all the time?" Gordy then grabbed Kellie and gave her another big hug. He could feel her shivering all over. Archie said, "Good work, mate. Is George fella still in one piece?"

"The yella fella hit George on the head with gun, George see many stars. What for they hit George so hard? Yella fella, real mean," said George. Gordy looked at Archie and said, "They smashed your radio up real bad and I don't think you can ever use it again. As a matter of fact it's nothing but junk now. I think it would be a smart idea if we move away from here as fast as possible. The Japanese are going to wonder what happened to their three soldiers and sooner or later they will send a lot more soldiers to find out."

Archie looked thoroughly disgusted, he said, "Well, I sure made a mess out of this effort, didn't I? If somebody didn't know for sure, they might just think I was working for the ruddy Nips. You're right, mate, without the radio we might just as well pack up and move out of here."

Gordy said, "I'll go and cover our tracks so that a dog could find them but no one else. I expect the Japanese will have trackers, so we will have to be very careful from now on. A lot will depend on how many soldiers they have to spare. I don't think they will be willing to risk fifty soldiers just to find three, not yet anyways."

George said, "You come village belong George, stay there at night, hide in bush in day. Gordy fella very brave, he save George from yella fellas, so George help Gordy fella." When Gordy came back from covering up any sign of a skirmish, they picked up everything and headed for George's village, As they approached the small village, Archie called a halt. He said, "I really don't think it is too smart to take this army stuff into the village, it's not new issue but it's still army. If the Nips show up and see it laying around, they could shoot everyone in sight just to be on the safe side. We can still see the village when we want to, but they can't see us." That turned out to be one of Archie's better ideas. When they had put everything completely out of sight, they went with George into the village.

It was time for the main meal of the day, so as honored guests they were naturally invited to join in. There were three different kinds of fish and many tropical fruits on the menu that day. The islanders have many ways to cook fruits and fish that have been handed down through generations. After they had eaten their fill, George stood up and called for their attention. Then he told everyone how his great friend and mighty hunter, Gordy fella, had rescued him from mean yella fellas. It was a battle equal to the First World War, the way George told it, even though he had been out like a light most of the time. The villagers asked Gordy to tell what happed, as he saw it.

Gordy knew he had to be very careful and diplomatic, he didn't want to make George look bad, or he could be losing a good friend just when he needed him. So Gordy started out by telling the villagers that the two Japanese soldiers had hit George fella over the head many times with their gun butts. Because they knew just by looking at George that he was a powerful fighter, the soldiers knew beyond a doubt that he would probably tear them both apart if they didn't knock him out fast, so they kept two armed soldiers there to guard him. The villagers all looked over at George fella with admiration, and he was sitting quite nonchalant with a big smile on his handsome face. Gordy could see that it was safe to tell the real story now; George fella's honor was now well established.

Gordy told them how he had crawled like a snake to get to the place where he could get the best shot. He knew he had to do it right the first time. There would be no second chance to pull off this rescue. Gordy explained that the two soldiers who were outside the hut were the closest together and if he could shoot them, he would have a much better chance. Every couple of minutes George would groan, so they were watching him very closely. Gordy said that he shot the two soldiers high on the chest so that they would fall backwards, making the third soldier, who was inside the hut, think that the enemy was in a treetop.

He explained to the villagers how he waited and waited for the third soldier to get out of the door. But the soldier refused to come out. He explained to the villagers that the yella fella could only do one other thing: make a hole in the foliage at the back of the little hut and try to sneak up on him. Gordy then showed them how the third soldier crawled along the ground, and how he raised his head to look at the treetops. Gordy had all the villagers holding their breath. When he described in great detail how the man's head came into his rifle sights, and how he squeezed the trigger so slowly, not even the dogs barked—they too felt the excitement.

The applause was loud and long. The villagers had seen an expert give a performance tonight and they showed their appreciation. Even old Archie McCauly, who thought he had seen just about everything, was impressed and gave Gordy a good rousing handclap. George fella was right in the center of the admiration that erupted from the villagers.

Kellie had not known exactly what had happened down at the hut, but she too was amazed at the way Gordy had handled the situation. She thought that Gordy seemed a little too bloodthirsty at times and it scared her a little. Archie and Gordy slept in one of the village huts that night and Kellie stayed with some of the younger "marys." They were so exhausted after all the excitement of the day, everyone slept like logs. After the Japanese patrol plane flew over early the next morning, they ate breakfast with the villagers. It consisted mainly of lots of strong tea and some fruit.

Gordy would have given an arm and a leg for a good feed of bacon and eggs smothered in hot cakes. The early morning patrol plane was like a alarm clock. It flew over the village at the same time every morning. They were not aware that the Japanese changed their schedule every ten to twelve days, just to throw off anyone who was counting on the patrol plane to be at a certain place, at a certain time.

Archie asked his friend George fella, "Could you get a big boat for Gordy, his mary, and myself? It would have to be big enough to carry much food for three people."

George said, "Gordy fella save George from mean yella fellas, so George will get boat for Gordy fella. Village belong my mary has big boat, George and mary will go now and be back in two days."

Archie, Gordy, and Kellie then made their way back to the camp where they had left their crates. BoBo showed up about an hour later and asked Gordy if he wanted to go hunt pig. Gordy asked BoBo if he had his dad's permission to go hunting. BoBo said he would go and ask him now. He whirled around and was gone on the run. In less than twenty minutes he was back with his dad's permission. Gordy got the rifle out and away they went. BoBo took Gordy in a different direction this time; he knew his dad didn't like him going into the place they were heading.

Dan knew there were some real soggy places in the area and one young boy was lost there, just a year ago. BoBo knew there were many pigs there and he wanted his friend Gordy fella to shoot a really big pig. It did not take long before the sound of pigs could be heard coming from a real swampy clearing.

Gordy didn't like the feeling of the ground beneath him and was just about ready to turn around when they heard the pigs. He told BoBo to move back as he squatted down. Gordy listened to the pigs grunting back and forth among themselves. He waited, listening carefully to each different grunt. Then he made a grunt. No noise came from the underbrush, so he grunted again. The bush parted, and there was a boar the size of a small horse. It grunted loudly and Gordy shot him right between the eyes. The huge boar dropped in his tracks. It kicked violently two or three times then stopped. Gordy cut it down the stomach and dumped the innards out just as he had done with the first pig. Then he and BoBo dragged the huge pig right to the village.

In a little over half an hour, Gordy and BoBo returned to where Kellie and Archie were. Kellie asked, "What happened, Gordy? Did the pigs hear that the big hunter was coming and run away?" She laughed and ran over and gave Gordy a big kiss, as a consolation prize.

BoBo started to laugh and said, "Gordy fella got big number-one pig, and take to village for kiki." BoBo laughed so hard he nearly fell down, then he said, "Now Gordy fella have to give Kellie back her kiss." BoBo couldn't stop laughing; he thought it was hilarious.

After the patrol plane had passed overhead on its way back to the airport, they made their way to the village. The meal that night was another feast of ham and many kinds of fruits. The feast lasted about an hour and a half of continuous stuffing. It was indeed a feast fit for a king. Now it was time for Gordy to get up and tell them how he was able to bag such a prize pig. Gordy told the villagers how easy it was to hunt the mighty porker with the great guide he had.

"My great guide, BoBo, led me right to the biggest pig in the whole area, maybe the whole island. Anyone can be a great hunter if he has a great guide. Only a fool turns down an offer from such a great guide." BoBo was not smiling so much that night because he knew he had disobeyed his dad. Dan didn't say anything or eat any of the pig that night, he quietly showed BoBo his displeasure at being disobeyed.

They slept in the village again that night. It was such a relief to get away from the bugs that fly and crawl around in the bush, in the darkness of the night. The air comes alive with the flying insects of every size and description as soon as the sun goes down. They went back to their camp after the patrol plane woke them in the morning. Archie made a billy of strong tea and they had some of the fruit the villagers had given them for breakfast. They sat on the crates and drank tea for a couple of hours. Archie told them some scary stories that had happened while he was managing plantations in the early days.

According to Archie, the natives would think nothing of going in to the mountains about once a year and battling the people there, bringing one or two back to eat later at the big victory feast. Of course sometimes it worked the other way around, the coast natives would be the main course at one of their celebrations. Apparently the plantation manager who had been there before Archie arrived disappeared one festive season and never was found.

Chapter Eight

Spare Coils

While he was telling them the stories of his early years on New Britain, Archie was sitting on one of the upturned crates. He could see the part of the village when he happened to look that way. All of a sudden he leaned forward as though not believing his eyes. Then he said, "Gordy, get the binoculars will you, mate? I have a hunch we might have some more visitors." Gordy dug out the glasses and handed them to Archie. After taking a quick look, Archie said, "Blimey, there are five of the little buggers this time!" Archie then gave the glasses to Gordy, who had slowly stood up. Then he carefully brought the binoculars up to eye level, he didn't want to make any fast moves that would draw any attention.

Gordy studied the whole compound for a good ten minutes. Finally he sat down again; for about five minutes he didn't say a word. He said, "For some reason they have all the villagers sitting in the middle of the compound. It's as though they expect a boat to arrive and pick them up. If the villagers are moved somewhere else we'll never be able to help them, Archie. We will have to do something drastic and do it fast, old timer." Gordy stood up again very slowly and once more he studied the compound. For a good five minutes he stared intently through the binoculars.

When he sat down, he put his hand on his chin as though he was deep in thought, then he said, "Archie, look into your tool box and see if they put any extra radio coils in there, will you? I don't know for sure if my idea will work, but as I said we have to try something. Our friend George won't be very happy with us, if he comes back with a boat and finds his family is gone."

Archie said, "There are two coils here, should I bring any of the other tools?" Gordy shook his head.

Gordy got two full clips for the rifle, then he gave Kellie a big hug and said, "Stay here, little one; don't come down there till I tell you." Gordy and Archie started carefully down the trail to the village, but after a minute, Gordy said, "Hold it, old-timer, I'll be right back." He returned to Kellie and gave her another big hug. She was so small and frightened he hated to leave her. Gordy held her tight and said, "Do not worry, little one, it will be all right, I am the 'Brother of the Bear'."

Then he turned around and took off down the path once more. *That will give her something to think about and chew over*, thought Gordy. He caught up with Archie once again in a couple of minutes. When they were closer to the village, they both got down on their bellies and crawled the last twenty feet.

"Well Archie, old trapper, now you will be glad you are small and scrawny," Gordy said. "I'm far too big to do what has to be done. This plan will have to work the first time, or we are sunk! If it works, Archie, you will be a hero, and if it doesn't, we will be in big trouble!"

Gordy really hated giving instructions to somebody as old as his dad, but he knew this old hunter's ploy would work if it were performed right. He said, "You will have to keep lower than a snake's belly, old-timer. To make this little trick work right, you are going to have to crawl around the entire village on your belly. Then you have to fasten the end of the coil-wire securely to one of the thin branches on that bush, way over on other side of the compound. Whatever you do, Archie, don't try to take a shortcut; we will only get one chance to make this plan work.

"Besides these soldiers probably aren't too well trained, so we just might have a chance. If we only had another rifle we would have a better chance, but unfortunately we don't. A lot will depend on how well you fasten the wire, mate; we don't want it breaking the branch off or coming undone. Be careful, Archie; and remember, don't try any shortcuts, whatever you do." Gordy felt funny after Archie crawled away into the undergrowth. He thought, *The old goat has probably been in ten times worse spots than I have ever been in. Thank God, he is a tough little character and doesn't mind using someone else's idea.*

At one point, one of the Japanese soldiers turned and looked hard at a spot between two of the huts. Gordy was sure the soldier must have spotted Archie! The soldier then turned to say something to one of the other soldiers, probably his sergeant. Gordy let out with a call of the Bird of Paradise. He had heard the natives make the call many times when they were high on Betel nuts. It is a loud, raucous, piercing call that scares the pants off you if you are not expecting it. The natives in the compound answered the call, convincing the soldier that it was probably a bird he had seen in the brush. Archie was well hidden by the time the soldier looked back.

When Archie finally got back to where Gordy was, he was wet with perspiration and looked like a dishrag. He said, "Lord love a duck, mate, that is one hell of a long way to go on one's belly, believe me! I didn't have any idea there was that much wire in one of those ruddy coils. I'll tell you this mate, I thought the blighters had me spotted one time, I was sure I had blown it again. Right away, I knew it was you that let out with that poor imitation birdcall."

Gordy looked at the scrawny little character; his tough old wrinkled face was a story in itself. Gordy said, "Well mate, let's get the show on the road. When you pull on that coil-wire, I hope the soldiers will shoot at the bush. When they fire, I will shoot the back ones first. With any kind of luck, we will get most of them before they even wake up to the fact that we are here. Go ahead, Archie, see if you can make that bush do a dance for our friends."

Archie gave the wire a good pull and one of the natives sitting on the ground pointed at the bush. The soldier closest to the bush yelled some command at it, then he raised his rifle. He yelled even louder in Japanese, then the soldier took aim and fired. Gordy fired at the same time. One of the soldiers in the back fell over. Then the rest of the soldiers thought for sure they were being attacked, so they immediately opened fire.

Gordy managed to shoot the four soldiers at the back before the last man tumbled to the fact that they were being shot at from behind. He turned around but it was too late; he was dead before he could get a single shot away. The natives sitting in the middle of the shooting were stunned and didn't move for several minutes. Then they got up and ran toward the bushes where Gordy and Archie were hiding.

The natives were excited and all talking at once. BoBo took a flying leap and jumped up on Gordy. He threw him into the air then caught him again and said, "BoBo, will you tell Kellie to come to village." As soon as Gordy has the words out of his mouth, BoBo was gone.

Archie was amazed at the way things had gone; it had all happened so fast. For the first few minutes he just stood still not saying a word. Then he said, "We must get rid of these dead soldiers fast as we can. We'll all be shot on the spot if any more Nips turn up while they are laying about. Why don't we put them in their own boat and send it out to sea." The Japanese soldiers had arrived in a shallow draft boat they use as a landing craft. Dan came up with a great idea of setting the boat on fire, so when it got out far enough, it would sink.

"Dan fella is one smart man. He is always coming up with good ideas and that is the best idea I have heard for a long time," Archie said. When the bodies of the soldiers were all on board, Gordy started the motor. All of the Japanese rifles also thrown into the craft—nothing was left to show that the soldiers had ever been there.

Gordy tied the crafts rudder amidships; he wanted to make sure that the boat would go straight out from the village. It would not be too good for them if the boat with the bodies washed ashore in a day or two. There was a spare can of petrol on board, so they dumped it over the dead Japanese soldiers. Archie took a tunic off one of the soldiers and doused it with petrol then he crammed the tunic into the bow and threw a match on it. Gordy put the motor into gear and they shoved the boat away from the little dock. Once the craft got out of the lee of the island and into the wind, the tunic started to burn like mad. The burning boat went out a long way and when it was nearly out of sight, the craft sank beneath the waves, leaving not a trace of its five occupants. An hour later a navy launch cruised slowly by the entrance to the small bay, the deck was lined with sailors scanning the shorelines with binoculars.

The feast in the village that night was really exciting and the villagers were all waiting for the story time afterward. They knew it was going to be a great performance when Gordy fella was telling the story. Archie was the first one to tell his part in the day's events. He went into great detail about crawling on his belly around the whole village to fasten the wire onto the bush. Archie was not the best storyteller in the world by any stretch of the imagination, but that night he had them hanging on every word.

Then Gordy got up and told the story once more, as only a great hunter can tell a story. Even the little kids sat still and hardly breathed. He described to the villagers how Archie crawled around the village and how he was nearly seen by one of the soldiers. Gordy then made the wild-bird call. He knew it was not perfect, but when the natives answered it, the Japanese were satisfied it was a bird in the bush. He told them how Archie fella made the bush dance to make the soldiers think that someone was hiding behind it. When the first soldier fired a warning shot, Gordy pretended to shoot one of the soldiers. Then the rest of the soldiers were sure they were under attack. He showed how he picked them off, one by one. The last soldier finally realized the shots were coming from behind. But it was too late. He never had time to get one shot away before he, too, joined his ancestors. Kellie listened to every word and was worried; Gordy seemed to enjoy killing a little too much.

That night Archie McCauly was a hero at last; never in his whole life had he been so revered as he was that night. The villagers came and thanked him one after the other. It was a great end to a hectic day, each villager saw the whole thing a little differently and they sat talking about the event for hours. Later it was agreed that Archie would sleep in the hut that George fella and his mary usually used. Gordy and Kellie were put in another hut by themselves. Before they turned in for the night they went for a walk along the beach. Kellie looked at Gordy in a strange way, and said, "Tell me, Gordon, why is it that you are so vicious at time and so gentle at other times? I don't understand it."

Gordy pondered the question, then said, "Little one, I learned from a great hunter that the Creator loves prey, just as much as he does the hunter.

I hold no bad feelings for my enemies. I know that each time I go into a dangerous situation where someone may be killed, there is a good chance that it may be me. I use all the skills I have been taught to make sure I'm not the victim. The Japanese soldiers are trained to fight hard and use their teachings to kill their enemies. I too was trained to hunt; only I had a better teacher."

The following morning the whole village slept late. The Japanese had decided to change the schedule that night, and consequently, the patrol plane didn't fly directly over the village. A young native girl ran into the hut Gordy and Kellie were in and yelled, "Wake up Gordy fella! Boat here now, with yella fellas!" Gordy quickly looked out the doorway and saw a small navy launch just getting to the jetty. The deck of the launch was crawling with Imperial Marines, and they swarmed ashore as soon as the boat touched the dock.

Gordy quickly made an opening through the foliage in the back of the hut, and they scampered through the hole as fast as they could. Gordy quickly pulled foliage back across the opening. Then he and Kellie both dived into the bush, trying their hardest not to make a sound. As fast as was possible they made their way back to where the crates were. Gordy got the rifle out and put a fresh clip into it. He kept mumbling to himself, "Blast it all, blast it all." He moved over a bit to where there was some heavier foliage, then he stood up with great care. Gordy slowly raised his head to see if he could find out what was happening in the compound. "Blast it all," he said again, then he sat down on the crate beside Kellie. He didn't say a word for minutes he didn't quite know how to tell her what he had seen.

"They have Archie," he finally said. "There is not a damn thing we can do about it; those sailors are Imperial Marines. They are the best and the toughest the Japanese have, not like those other poorly trained soldiers. I know Archie would not want us to risk our lives and the lives of people in the village by doing something reckless trying to rescue him. Those marines are really the cream of the Japanese military, believe me. We wouldn't have a chance against that many of them." Gordy stood up and watched as the sailors ran from hut to hut, looking for other white people. The marines had herded all the natives over to one side of the compound and completely ignored them. They were looking for white people; they didn't have anything else on their minds.

When the marines roughly dragged Archie onto the small dock, he suddenly lashed out with his one foot and kicked one of the marines off the jetty. One of the other sailors immediately hit Archie over the head with his rifle butt. Poor Archie went down like a sack of potatoes. The marine who hit him then picked Archie up by his belt and literally threw him onto the deck of the launch. The marine Archie had kicked off the dock scrambled from the water and then made a mad dash to get onto the launch as it left the dock.

Kellie sobbed, "What will they do to him, Gordy? He is an old man and he's not in the army; what harm could an old man like Archie do them any way?"

Gordy knew that poor old Archie was doomed, there was no use beating around the bush. He said, "The main trouble is that Archie is white. If the Japs are going to have any success in these countries, they must prove the whites can be beaten. They will probably put Archie on some kind of trial, then sentence him to death. If Archie is lucky, he will be taken out and shot." Gordy secretly thought that they would probably decapitate him in the middle of the cricket grounds on a Saturday afternoon. That grisly thought he didn't think wise to relate to Kellie.

Gordy didn't think it would be too smart to go back to the village just yet. The villagers needed some time to settle down and talk things over among themselves. He realized that if the little native girl had not come to their hut first, they would be the ones in big trouble right now. There probably wouldn't have been enough time to keep Kellie from falling into Japanese hands. Once again the grisly thought came to Gordy, *What if they were about to be taken prisoner; could I possibly put a bullet into Kellie?* He sure hoped he never had to find out. The thought of it bothered him nearly to distraction. Gordy decided to keep the rifle close at all times and loaded, just in case. Slitting her throat would be too difficult; he was sure he couldn't do that. Kellie looked at Gordy, as though she knew what he had been thinking and she shuddered. With Archie gone now, what on earth would she do if anything happened to Gordy?

Dan fella came to see them at noon and he looked so sad. It seemed odd to see him without a big smile on his handsome face. He just stood and stared at the ground for a long while before he spoke. "Yella fellas come and take Archie fella away. People belong village belong Dan, very very sad, Archie fella old friend. People belong village have no gun, so can't fight yella fellas."

Gordy could see the pain on the usually happy face of this beautiful man. He said, "Dan fella, we saw what happened at the village this morning; we saw sailors take Archie fella away. Archie fella would not want Dan's people to be hurt. Dan and George fella's family are just like his own family, and he would be very sad if they were hurt trying to help him. Those yella fellas, very bad."

Dan then said, "Gordy and mary come to village for kiki, better come when sun go down. Then no more yella fellas come to village. Dan's people very very sad; they no able to help old friend Archie fella." Dan then left with a miserable look still on his face. After the Japanese patrol plane went over late in the day, Gordy and Kellie made their way to the small village. All of the people came up to them one after the other and told them how sad they were and that they didn't know how to help their old friend, Archie fella.

After a meal of fish and many different kinds of fruit, they sat around and drank tea. It was not the happy feast of previous nights by any stretch of the imagination. The villagers felt their new friend Gordy fella might think they were not brave and courageous. After the meal Gordy got up and spoke to the people of the village. He said, "Don't feel bad that you could not help your old friend today. Archie fella would feel very bad if his friends were killed, or even hurt, trying to help him. Many times Archie fella told me that the people of village were like his family. I know that Archie fella very glad that there were no guns in the village, or many of his friends wouldn't be here tonight. Those yella fellas that came this morning, very bad." Gordy could say no more so he sat down.

Gordy and Kellie slept in the hut again that night but it was an uneasy sleep. Early the next morning they had some tea and fruit in the village, then they went back to where the crates were. About two hours later the day started to heat up. Kellie said, "Why don't we go down to the water's edge? The flies are going to drive us batty if we stay here. We don't have to go too far from the village and we can stay a lot cooler."

"That's a real good idea," Gordy said. "I'll take the binoculars with us, and if we see any Jap boats we can always hide in the bush till they leave. I think we had better go to the village first and tell Dan where we are going." They packed the binoculars and took some fruit for their lunch. Gordy checked the rifle over and took two extra clips of shells with him. He was slowly coming to realize that the Japanese were not a very predictable lot. As they passed through the village they stopped and told Dan what they had planned to do.

Dan said, "George fella be back today with big boat, the people of village get many fruit for Gordy fella. Also we catch many fish for Gordy fella, to take for kiki." Then Dan told them about a nice cool beach about two miles away from the village. Gordy found the beach Dan had told them about. It was a popular place for the people of the village because the wind was always blowing strong enough to keep the flies away, and the water just the right temperature. They both waded into the water up to their waists, and it was so refreshing. Gordy kept a sharp eye out for sharks, which thrive in the waters around New Britain.

Later in the afternoon when Gordy was scanning the sea with binoculars, he said, "I think I see a small sail on the end that little atoll. It's hard to make out but I'm sure it's a sail." He handed the glasses to Kellie and she looked as hard as she could, but she couldn't even see atoll for a good five minutes. Then she finally saw the small atoll and also spotted the bright-colored sail. As Kellie was scanning the sea, Gordy was standing a little behind her. Looking at her trim figure in the short sarong started a whole troupe of gerbils racing around his brain.

The little sarong the native ladies had given her looked very tempting indeed. Gordy started thinking it might not look too bad hanging from a tree for an hour or two. Gordy's vivid imagination suddenly took over, and suddenly they were myriads of damsels in tiny sarongs, dancing around his head. When Kellie turned around to say something, she saw the funny look on Gordy's face. What he had on his mind right then was not too hard to figure out!

Kellie said, "That must be George all right. I think we had better get back to the village before one of us gets hit on the noggin with a pair of binoculars." They gathered up the things they had brought with them and started back along the beach. Kellie said, "You go first, Gordon, I really don't know if I like the way you are looking at me today. You look like you want to play Tarzan and Jane, or doctor and patient maybe. Or do you have some of your own sailor games?"

Gordy smiled and didn't say a word but he thought, *Little one, if we don't get off this island soon, someone is going to play something. You can bet your booties on that.*

By the time Gordy and Kellie got back to the village, George and his mary were just coming into the jetty. They had brought a large ceremonial catamaran from his mary's village. Dan helped tie up the big canoe, then he talked to his brother George. Quietly he told George what had happened while he was gone. Gordy and Kellie kept well in the background, while the two brothers talked things through. George finally came over to where they were standing and told them, "Gordy fella and mary must leave when sun goes down; it is very bad here for white fellas. George so sorry about old friend Archie fella. Archie fella and George, friends long long time. After kiki, Gordy fella must leave village belong George and Dan. George have very very bad day; he lose many friends today." George then spent a couple of hours telling Gordy how the people of the region navigate by the sun and the stars. It sounded so easy the way George explained it.

George explained to Gordy that the first couple of days would be the most dangerous. He also suggested that if they could still see the island when the sun came up on the second day, he should take down the sail. The yella fella's airplane could see the sail for many miles, but not the boat. If the sail was seen by the yella fellas, Gordy and mary would be in big trouble. Once Gordy fella no longer could see island, they should be safe.

The people of the village helped to load the catamaran by stuffing dried fish and fruit into every nook and cranny they could find. Every family of the village contributed what ever they could to the food supply. They knew the chances of Gordy fella and his mary reaching their destination were very slim. The women of the village gave Kellie a gourd of coco-butter to rub on herself so that the sun wouldn't cook her to a frazzle. They also gave her a woven wide-brimmed hat that she could tie on. Both these gifts would prove to be lifesavers.

The meal that night was not the joyous festival of other nights. It dragged on and on, with very little laughing and chatter. After the meal, every member of the village came forward to say their goodbyes. BoBo was very sad to see his big friend leave. He thanked Gordy fella for showing him how to hunt pigs. There were tears rolling down his handsome little face, as he said goodbye. Dan then brought out Archie's old Australian army hat, which had been left behind when the marines dragged him away. It was a very solemn and powerful moment, when Dan fella made the presentation to Gordy.

The sun was going down now, and the patrol plane had gone over the village a good half an hour ago. It was nearly time to leave, and Gordy was having second thoughts about his ability to sail to Australia. Suddenly he realized that he knew very little about sailboats. He started to wonder if they could hide out in the bush till the war was over. He knew the Japanese were bound to find out that there was a white man hiding somewhere, and they would come after him. Gordy knew that most of the natives got on well with the whites, but there were a few who hated the white people. They would turn the whites into the Japanese at the first chance they got. Gordy realized it was a leave now, or never.

The whole village came down to the small jetty and watched as Gordy and Kellie climbed in among the foodstuff. When they were sitting in the right spot and ready to go, George untied the lines. The catamaran moved away from the dock very slowly at first. It was as if it didn't want to leave this land of warm gentle people any more than they did. When they got out a little farther, the trade winds suddenly caught the sail and the catamaran began to pick up speed. Gordy had not handled a sailboat for many years, and even then he had only sailed a couple of times. George had told Gordy to sail straight out from the village; he mustn't let the boat drift one way or the other.

Early the following morning, just before the sun came up (according to George), they should reach a very small island. On the other side of the tiny atoll they would find a strip of sandy beach. Gordy would have to pull the boat up onto the sand and they would have to hide there until the sun went down the next day. They skipped across the waves at a good clip and the night became darker as the stars became brighter, There were so many stars in the jet-black sky that every time Gordy turned his head he lost the star he was steering by. It sounded so easy when George was telling him how to do it. One thing George had neglected to tell him was how to tell one blasted star from another. There were literally billions of stars in the heavens. Gordy finally found one star that was a little brighter than the rest, and he kept that one at the top of the mast. Gordy knew if they missed this little spit of an island, they would wind up in the main shipping lanes and the Japanese would then spot them for sure.

The noise of the water splashing against the canoe's hull sounded so assuring to Kellie. She would turn around and look at Gordy and think, *The big bloke might get me home after all. He really is something out of the box and I wish I really knew how he felt about me.* Kellie dropped off to sleep two or three times during the night, but Gordy didn't dare. All night long he kept looking at the mast and the star he had picked. Every once in a while he would lower his eyes to give them rest. When Gordy looked back at the top of the mast, he would wonder for a minute if he was still looking at the same star.

Two or three times he got panicky and he would try to find the star he had been looking at, then he would realize he was all right. He would give a big sigh of relief when he realized the mast was still on the proper star. Gordy knew that the ocean's currents would make a large ship drift miles off course. What it would do to a small sailboat, he didn't have a clue. Another thing, he never knew a night could be so blasted long. He wanted to close his eyes in the worst way, but he dare not. The trade winds never slackened or changed direction once, and he never had to adjust the sail once. That suited Gordy just fine. The last thing he wanted to do was start changing the sail around in the middle of a pitch-black night.

He didn't dare let Kellie think he was a bit doubtful about them finding their target. He was actually glad she was not awake, asking him a bunch of questions he didn't want to answer. The night dragged on and on and his eyes were getting sore from staring at the top of the mast. Then he thought he saw a black mass appearing out of the darkness dead ahead. He waited another twenty minutes and there it was, the little island. Kellie was stirring a bit and she asked him if he thought there were still on course. "That's the island, little one, dead ahead," he said.

Kellie sat up then and was excited as a kid in a candy store. They had passed the first test with no trouble at all. Kellie started acting as though they were practically sailing into Sydney Harbour. She said, "Don't you think that is a good sign, Gordy? We found the first place without any trouble at all, and we can't get to Aussie unless we do it a bit at a time. I think it's a good sign, anyway."

Gordy steered the catamaran around to the other side of the tiny atoll where, just as George had said, there was a small beach. They pulled the catamaran as far as they could up the sandy slope. Gordy then took the sail off the boat and covered the hull with some of the dry palm leaves, which littered the ground. He took the sail among the twenty odd palm trees on the little atoll, laid it out, and they used it as a mattress. They were both just dozing off for a much-needed sleep, when the Japanese patrol plane flew overhead.

It was a good four or five hours later when Kellie woke up. She looked around and nearly died of fright. Not more than five hundred yards away was what looked like to her the largest battleship in the world. Its huge guns were aiming right at the little island, and Kellie was sure they were getting ready to fire. "Gordy, wake up, for God's sake! Gordy, wake up!" she cried. Gordy woke up and looked out past Kellie. *Suffering bowling balls,* he thought. He had seen a few large ships in his day but never anything like this huge battleship. Gordy grabbed Kellie's arm and said, "Don't move an inch Kellie, don't even blink your eyes. If we stay perfectly still they won't spot us." She wanted to crawl under the sail in the worst way, but she didn't.

Then, what appeared to be a brand new Japanese destroyer suddenly arrived on the scene. It was a sleek deadly looking craft, passing between the atoll and the battleship. Gordy figured the destroyer was making over forty knots, at least. He had never seen a ship of its size going that fast. The huge battleship turned ever so slowly, then both ships headed north. In about fifteen minutes both ships were out of sight, but it took a good hour for the scare to wear off.

The day passed slowly and they had some dried fish and fruit for lunch. Every bite was eaten slowly and one small cup of water each, finishing off the meal. After eating they scrounged the atoll for more food, but there was none. There were a lot of bird's nests all over the place, but they didn't have any birds or eggs in them. The palm trees were also bare of coconuts. Gordy didn't know much about the coconut palms, but he did hear someone say that they had to be a certain age before they bore coconuts. These trees apparently weren't old enough, or else it was the wrong time of year. It looked like they were out of luck at finding something to add to their meager food supply.

It was Kellie who saw the large turtle first. The poor thing was injured badly, it seemed like one of its back legs was missing completely. Gordy immediately thought, *It probably tangled with the propeller on that Japanese destroyer.* The turtle was trying its hardest to get up on the beach, so Gordy went down and helped it. The poor creature was almost dead and Kellie asked, "How can we help the poor thing, Gordon?"

"Easy," said Gordy. He took his knife and cut the creature's head off. He then tossed the head back in to the water. Kellie looked absolutely disgusted! Gordy said, "It was in agony and suffering, it would have died soon." Kellie was going to say something like, *I suppose if I was ruddy well suffering, you would cut my head off, wouldn't you.* But she thought that she might not like the answer she got, so she kept quiet.

Gordy scraped a hole in the sand, then he rolled the turtle on its side and propped it there. He had a real tough job cutting through the thick skin on the turtle's underside. He then let the innards fall into the small pit in the sand. Gordy then turned the turtle back onto its broad shell. Kellie looked at the whole operation with a sickly look on her face. Right then, she didn't really think they were that hard up for food. Gordy asked, "Kellie, will you go and get some of those bird nests and bring them here?" He could plainly see that Kellie did not enjoy this part of the surviving in the wilds. Gordy had never cooked a turtle before in his life. He had never seen one cooked. He had heard that the natives ate them with great relish. Of course they eat anything with great relish, he realized.

Kellie brought him a couple of the bird's nests and asked, "Where do you want these put?"

"Lay them right on top of the turtle, will you? We will need every nest you can find before it's fully cooked," said Gordy. He took the binoculars out of the canoe and removed one of the front lenses. In a few minutes, the sun focused through the thick lens and had the straw and twigs burning briskly. The twigs were all bone dry and made no smoke, which was a good thing. The dried foliage burned at a very fast rate, and kept them hustling just to keep the fire from going out. Gordy and Kellie gathered up every nest on the atoll and put them on the fire. Soon the heat from the fire was so intense that it made them back away. When all of the bird's nests were gone, they put the dry palm leaves onto the fire. Eventually the fire died out, but the turtle shell was still very hot; they couldn't even touch it. Gordy climbed up some of the trees and gathered some green leaves to wrap the strange-looking meat in.

The turtle meat looked and felt like hard gray rubber now that it was cooked. Gordy sure hoped it tasted a lot better than it looked. Gordy knew the islanders had been eating turtles since the dawn of history and they sure didn't look like they had suffered. Maybe the natives know something about cooking turtles that he never heard of. He sure wished George or Dan were here so he could ask them. When they had all the strange-looking meat stuffed into the canoe, they lay down again for another nap. Gordy knew it would be another long night ahead of them and as George said, they had to be out of sight of the island when the sun came up or else the patrol plane might spot them.

Three hours later they woke up and had some fish and a little fruit; again they only allowed themselves one small cup of water each. Gordy was still hungry as a bull-moose after their little snack. He wasn't sure he was gong to be able to eat so little food each day. He could understand Kellie only eating a spoonful of food every few hours. She was only the size of a pigmy anyway, but eating made him hungry. Even thinking of eating made him hungry, and he knew it was going to be a tough job not to eat more than his share.

For some strange reason he started to wonder what his old friend Charley would say if he were here. He wished he could ask him how to handle a situation like this. Gordy thought, *He would probably look at me with an understanding look, then he would probably say, "No use thinking of food, when you don't have any, my young friend. Wait till your larder is full."* It made him feel a little more secure just thinking of old Charley. Beyond a doubt, the things he had learned from Charley had got them where they were. He also knew that if they were going to make it back to Aussie, it would be because of the things his old Indian friend had taught him.

Chapter Nine

The Coral Sea

Just as the sun was going down, the Japanese patrol plane flew directly over the tiny atoll. The pilots used the small island as a marker to
check their heading back to the base. Gordy and Kellie had another cup of
water and some fruit for their last meal of the day. They had the sail up and
put back onto the catamaran within ten minutes after the plane disappeared
form view. Kellie squeezed herself into the canoe and Gordy shoved them
off the beach; the trade winds caught the sail almost immediately. After a little sail adjusting, away they went. It made them both feel good, like they
were on the last leg of a great journey.

The sun was just below the horizon and they could still see the glow in
the sky where it had been. George had told Gordy that he had to keep the
sun on his right shoulder when it went down, and on his left shoulder when
it came up. Gordy again searched the heavens for a star that was slightly
brighter than all the rest, to keep at the top of the mast. All night they went
up and down on the never-ending swells, for the first three or four hours it
was exciting. Kellie dozed off after awhile, and Gordy was left with the stars,
the ocean, and his thoughts. He had gotten Kellie away from the island; that
part of the rescue had succeeded fairly well. This next part he realized, may
be a lot tougher. The sail was filled to capacity all the time and they traveled
at a steady speed. The trade winds never varied in direction or velocity, and
Gordy was so glad of that.

The blackness of the night gradually began to diminish and the light of
day was trying to take over once more. When the first rays of daylight came,
they could still see New Britain on the horizon. He remembered that

George said, the great decorated sail would stand out like a sore thumb on the dark blue ocean. After all they had been through, he didn't think it very wise to take a chance now. Even with the sail down the ocean swells still moved them along at a fair clip.

Two hours later the island was out of sight and they felt a little safer. Gordy knew that a plane flying at a high altitude might still spot them, but he hoped for the best. When Gordy put the sail up once more, they could feel the catamaran pick up speed immediately. The wind got a lot warmer as the day wore on, and they knew that it was going to be a lot hotter before the sun set. All day they went up and down on the never-ending great blue swells. It was like being on a giant roller coaster. The wide-brimmed hats the natives had given them were a real Godsend.

The small meals they ate were made into a big event. They tried to make the fruit and one cup of water stretch out for a good hour or more. Time seemed to drag by so slowly. Gordy carved a little cut in the outrigger stay to mark the end of each long day. If he had not done that, the days would have started running into each other and they would not have known when to change direction. George had told Gordy that he must change course on the beginning of the day after the eleventh moon. It was only at the end of the third day, when Gordy said, "Kellie, I think maybe we had better start eating some turtle meat, it will make the other supplies last a lot longer."

Gordy cut off a piece of the funny-looking meat and he handed it to Kellie, who looked at it for a minutes then put it in her mouth. She had a real queer look on her face and she chewed about six times, then threw up. "Oh my giddy aunt! That is the worst tasting stuff I have ever eaten!" Kellie cried. "My God, you can't even chew the weird stuff; it's like chewing on a blasted rubber glove. It's ruddy well the most horrible tasting stuff I have ever tried to eat. Ugh, it's horrible."

Gordy thought, *Lord love a blasted duck, we have about forty pounds of the blasted stuff and it makes her sick.* He was sitting staring at the gray meat, when his thoughts drifted to the time when he and Charley had been out in the woods for weeks. They were very low on food and had found a dead moose. The wolves had been eating on the old carcass, so Charley cut off a piece of the meat. Later, when they stopped for the day, he built a fire and boiled the meat. Then he cooked it well on a spit.

After they had eaten the old moose meat, Charley had told Gordy, "The dog people are very smart and they have been around for a long time before humans arrived on the scene. They usually don't eat anything that will make them sick. If the dog people eat it, you too can eat it. Only you may have to boil it first, just to be on the safe side. Also remember my young friend, there are no tasters in your gut. When you have to eat bad stuff, you have to think of good things." Many times Gordy would think of that old piece of moose meat when he had to eat something he didn't want to eat or didn't taste very good.

Gordy cut off apiece of the rubbery turtle meat and stuck it in his mouth. Kellie was right, it had the taste of an old gum-boot and was almost as hard to chew. Gradually he got it down, then he cut off another piece of the gray meat and started to chew it. Kellie watched him and said, "Doesn't that horrid stuff make you gag? I have never tried to eat anything like that in my life. You're not forcing yourself to eat the terrible stuff just because it makes me sick, are you?"

"No, little one. As a matter of fact it tastes a little like old moose meat," said Gordy. "But I admit, you do have to acquire a taste for it. Don't you worry, I'll eat the turtle meat if you want to eat the fish and fruit. That way, they will both last a little longer." The days seemed to drag on and on endlessly. Each day seemed so much hotter than the day before and there was nothing to break up the scenery. If they could only see a bird, or even a blasted cloud, it would break up the time a little, but there was nothing. The boiling hot sun day after bloody day nearly drove them insane. They were both as brown as natives by now, and poor Kellie looked like a scarecrow. Her big, beautiful brown eyes looked so much bigger and almost had a haunting look to them now. Kellie had lost so much body mass by now that she looked even more gaunt than she really was.

On the tenth day they woke up to find a bank of clouds on the horizon, and they both got excited just seeing the clouds. They had almost forgot what clouds looked like. The clouds kept coming their way and they could feel the temperature going down as the clouds got closer. The wind died completely just before the deluge of water hit them. They stood up and tried to drink the rain as fast as it came down, but that proved useless. Then they tried to catch some of the rain in the empty gourds but that didn't work either. Gordy freed the port line on the sail and tipped up the other end. The water then ran off the sail as if it was coming out of a spout, and the four gourds were filled in a matter of minutes.

Then the deluge stopped suddenly and the wind picked up again. It all happened so fast that Gordy was caught off guard. The sail whipped around the mast and nearly sent Gordy overboard. The stern outrig stabilizer was the only thing that saved him from going over the side. Gordy held onto the sail for all he was worth. If the sail had gotten loose, it would have torn the mast right out of the canoe. With a mighty effort he got the port lines fast again, and he fell back completely exhausted. For almost two hours Gordy didn't move. The effort had sapped every ounce of strength out of him.

Kellie perked up a little bit after a couple cups of rainwater. What little dried fish they had left certainly wasn't dry anymore. Gordy realized it would rot real fast, so they agreed that Kellie should eat most of the fish that

71

day. The fruit supply was not much good either, but there was still enough for three or four days if they were careful.

The following day was extremely hot and steamy. The air literally sucked the little bit of energy they had left right out of them. Gordy reminded Kellie four or five times that tomorrow was the day that they changed course for Australia. Most of the time now, poor Kellie was silent. He big beautiful eyes were getting very dull and listless. Gordy would try his hardest to keep her talking, but she would often fall asleep in the middle of a word.

Gordy thought, *What I would do if Kellie didn't wake up one day?* He looked at her every few minutes and didn't think she was going to last too much longer. George had asked Gordy before they left the island if he would be able to eat Kellie if she died first. Gordy remembered that George was completely serious when he asked the question. He looked at Kellie again and thought, *There is nothing to eat now, she would hardly make a good sandwich.* He knew he couldn't do such a thing anyway, unless he went stark raving mad.

Early the next day, Gordy counted up the cuts on the establisher bar. He figured that it was the morning after the eleventh moon, and they should alter course. Now they should be heading straight for Australia, and that made Kellie perk up a bit. Gordy got Kellie to try the turtle meat once more. He cut the meat in very small bits that she could practically swallow without chewing. Kellie's taste buds had been dying a little each day, so she got a small bit of meat down. Later that same day he got another little bit of meat into her mouth. The problem now was to keep her awake long enough to swallow it.

The days went by in a fuzzy blur. They would come to, then drift off into a trance again after ten to fifteen minutes. Sometimes they would say a few words to each other, not often. Gordy eventually lost track of all time. The turtle meat was almost gone and they had only one swallow of water a day. The only thing they could do now was to keep sailing till they hit land. The boiling sun each day was drying them up like prunes, and the air was only a little cooler at night. Kellie would shiver like a dog at night, even though it was still hot as Hades as far as Gordy was concerned.

Eventually the food was all gone! Gordy had given the larger share of the turtle meat to Kellie once she had managed to get the first few swallows down. Gordy found it easier each time to get her to eat the weird stuff. He would pretend he was chewing on a piece of the meat, but he wouldn't actually put it in his mouth. The terrible pains of hunger Gordy had felt for the first couple of weeks had disappeared. Now the food and water were all gone, and he knew it was only a matter of time till they perished. There was just nothing they could do about it!

Chapter Ten

The *Croydon*

One extremely hot night, Gordy had finally drifted off into tormented sleep, and he dreamt once more of his old Indian friend Charley. It was the funniest thing, because in the dream, Charley was trying to say something to him. In his trancelike condition, Gordy was trying hard to hear what Charley was saying. He wasn't sure, but he thought he heard Charley say, "You are Brother of the Bear, and he will look after you, my young friend." Gordy shook his head to try to clear it so he could hear better, but he soon drifted off again.

Approximately two hours later, Gordy was awakened from his erratic sleep by a bump on the hull of the canoe. It took him a while to come awake. He really wasn't sure he felt a bump or he had dreamt about it. Gordy closed his eyes again and didn't wake again for half an hour. He was having such a hard time staying awake now, and poor Kellie was asleep most of the time.

It was broad daylight now. Kellie still had not stirred, so Gordy tried his best to wake her. It took some time for her to come around, but she eventually opened her eyes. Poor Kellie couldn't even talk anymore. She would just look at Gordy with deep brown expressionless eyes. Gordy did all the talking now. He would say over and over, "Hold on, little one, remember we are one day closer to home. Just try to hold on another day, Kellie, we will make it little one, I know it!"

Kellie was awake by then and facing the stern, he noticed that she seemed to be staring at something. Gordy moved his hand on front of Kellie's eyes. He thought maybe she couldn't see, but she blinked her eyes, so he knew her eyes were working. Gordy slowly turned his head, and there not more than a hundred yards away was the conning tower of a submarine. His first thoughts were, *It's a bloody Japanese sub!* Gordy shuddered in disbelief as the submarine got bigger. He knew he had to act fast. He couldn't let them take Kellie alive; not after all she had been through. Everything was a bit fuzzy and he grabbed the mast. The catamaran was nearly being tipped over. One of the four men on the bridge of the sub yelled, "Ahoy there! Do you need help?" Gordy waved his arm in the come-here fashion; that's all he could do. He couldn't have yelled to save his life.

After a lot of shouting and movement on the conning tower, a hatch suddenly opened and four men and an officer came up onto the lower deck of the sub. One of the men let a rope ladder over the side of the submarine and made it fast. Then another man threw over a heaving line, which Gordy wrapped around the mast of the catamaran, so the sailors could pull the canoe in real close. By this time Kellie was out like a light again. Gordy threw her over his shoulder and stepped onto the ladder hanging down the hull of the sub.

The sailors grabbed Gordy so he wouldn't fall. Then they pulled them both aboard the sub. Gordy wouldn't let go of Kellie. He even went down the hatch with her draped across his shoulder. At the bottom of the ladder an officer, who happened to be the second mate, told Gordy, "Follow me, mate, we have cabin for you and the young lady."

Gordy followed the officer down the narrow alleyway to a small cabin containing two bunks. They went in and Gordy gently put Kellie down on one of the bunks. She could not have weighed more than seventy pounds by this time. "The ship's doctor will be here in a minute or two," said the officer. Just as the second mate was about to back out of the cabin, another man came in. The second mate said, "This is the ship's doctor, Penrose; he will look after you." The doctor glanced quickly at Gordy and said, "You look like you will last awhile, mate. I think we had better check out the young lady first."

Then the doctor pried Kellie's eyes open and felt for her pulse. Immediately he rang the buzzer for the ship's steward. In about a minute the steward came into the room. The doctor told him, "Tom old man, will you get me a pitcher of tomato juice and put a jar of honey in it, and then mix them up really well. I don't want it cold but I do want it as fast as you can get it here." Tom left on the run. He and the bones were old friends and had sailed together before.

Dr. Penrose could easily see that the girl was in very fragile condition. He filled the little sink with warm water, then he washed Kellie's face and arms. Tom came back in minutes with a big pitcher of tomato juice and honey. Dr. Penrose put a little of the mixture in a cup and managed to get a couple of sips into Kellie. He left Kellie for a few minutes to give Gordy a quick once-over. Then for almost two days the doctor sat beside Kellie's bunk, waking her up every fifteen minutes to feed her more juice and honey. Ever so slowly the juice and honey began to do its work and Kellie began to come back to life. The doctor could see her resting more easily and her eyes becoming clearer by the hour. He knew it had been a close call for this girl. *It was really a wonder she survived this long,* he thought.

On the second day of sitting by Kellie's bunk, the doctor was startled when Gordy suddenly woke up from a dead sleep and wondered where he was. The doctor assured Gordy he was safe and sound. He poured him out a drink of juice and honey, which he drank and went right back to sleep. The ship's bell would ring again in an hour, and Gordy would come wide awake again and wonder where he was. Once more the doctor would assure him he was safe, and also that Kellie was fine.

Once Kellie was stable, the doctor gave Gordy an examination and he decided that all Gordy's big frame really needed was food, and lots of it. Gordy slept for nearly three days. The doctor thought that was the best medicine he could prescribe. He didn't think it odd that Gordy would wake up just long enough to make sure Kellie was all right. It simply proved that his mental condition was functioning and he was sure that when he had enough sleep, Gordy would wake up. Every hour the ship's bell would ring and Gordy would wake up and have a drink, then go back to sleep. It was almost humorous. Late on the third day Gordy woke up for good. Very hungry of course, but wide awake.

Dr. Penrose knew it had been a close call for both of these young people. He was sure that after another twenty-four hours without food and water, the young lady certainly would not have made it. The young man could have lasted no more than a week, at most. On the afternoon of the fourth day, Kellie came around. She wanted a cup of tea first thing and something to eat. Dr. Penrose took that as a real good sign. He had the steward bring her a cup of tea and some bread with vegimite spread on it.

The next day Kellie had a shower, while Gordy stood outside. A spare sailor uniform was found in the ship's slop-chest for Kellie. There were no uniforms that would fit Gordy, so one of the engine room crew volunteered to wash his clothes for him. By the next morning they were ready to be worn again. It had been a good month since Gordy had clean clothes on. They felt so good and he thanked the sailor three or four times.

Gordy didn't know that Kellie had told the doctor about him coming back to Rabaul to rescue her, and how he had single-handedly killed eight Japanese soldiers. The doctor had naturally told his old friend the second mate, who of course told the captain. A ship at sea is something like a small town ashore. There is just no way you can keep a secret or any news to yourself. Every little scrap of information is passed from one crew member to the next on their lonely, boring watches. They talk about absolutely everything under the sun, and nothing is sacred. A story like this was the best medicine in the world for the boredom that gets sailors into trouble. Sailors go bananas when they get ashore, because of the boredom they put up with at sea.

By the sixth day Gordy and Kellie were back on their feet, more or less, and eating regular meals served in the cabin. The second mate came into the cabin that afternoon and told them, "Captain Finch would like you both to join him for dinner in the main mess. He would like it, if both of you would sit at his table." By the time they walked into the mess that night everyone in the crew from the galley-man to the captain had heard the story. They all certainly didn't believe the story, but they had heard it. The whole crew gave Gordy and Kellie a standing ovation as they walked into the mess. Men who spent their lives in submarines don't usually get too pumped up about many things. Over the years they get accustomed to the strange happenings of man and nature.

The ship's crew had never seen one person stow away so many groceries at any one time. Gordy had a whole peach pie for afters and he drank a quart of milk to help wash it down. Some of the crew thought that watching Gordy eat was going to be the main entertainment for the evening. Gordy's taste buds had almost forgotten what real good food tasted like. The doctor had advised Kellie not to overload her stomach at first, but he knew Gordy's big frame needed food, so he didn't say anything to him. The crew more or less all sighed a great sigh of relief when Gordy finally put down his eating utensils. They all laughed when Gordy thanked the cook for the third time.

After the meal was finished and the dinner things were cleared away, the cups and coffee pots were placed on the mess-room tables. The captain then stood up and asked for the attention of every one. He stood and bowed his head a minute trying to think of the proper way to express what he wanted to say. The captain started by saying, "As you crew members all know, I am Captain Finch of the Royal Navy, and skipper of this submarine. I'm sure you would want to join me, as part of the crew of His Majesty's Submarine, *Croydon*, and take this opportunity to toast a real live hero. It is not too often we get this chance." With that, the captain and crew stood and drank to the health of Kellie and Gordy.

Captain Finch again hesitated a moment, trying to think of the right words. Then he said, "We have been on this milk run for almost a year now. We make our way through the Coral Sea, then zigzag our way back. Then it's back to Freemantle, and a week ashore for all hands. After that, we go back once more on the blasted milk run. We have not so much as seen an enemy ship, or fired one ruddy torpedo. I really think that the navy brass have lost their marbles sometimes, and other times I know it."

The captain continued, "I'm sure boredom is the main enemy of people serving in the submarine service. The navy records are filled with stores of well-balanced men who have gone bananas while serving in submarines.

Even high-ranking officers have been pushed over the edge while on long runs in these tin cans. Sometimes I have wished the crew would mutiny, just to break up the boredom. Of course, gentlemen, you know I'm only joking. I wouldn't like this conversation to get ashore." The crew all had a laugh over the captain's little joke.

The captain continued, "On this run, gentlemen, we have been rewarded by being part of a truly great adventure. The crew and I have heard some of this amazing story. It really seems too utterly bizarre to believe; it is like the script of a movie. Never have I been part of such an incredible rescue, and I would love to hear the complete story."

It took a minute before the captain went on, then he said, "I wonder if we can possibly get our guest to do us the honor and tell us the real story, as it actually happened. Just so we can tell our families when we get ashore." The captain looked over at Gordy, and the crew gave Kellie and Gordy another standing ovation.

Gordy then stood up and looked over at Kellie. She no longer looked like a skeleton, and her big brown eyes were alive again thanks to the good doctor, who had worked so hard to help Kellie recover her health. Gordy realized that they owed their lives to the crew of this British submarine, so he thought they deserved a bit of excitement to say the least.

Gordy stood quietly at the end of the captain's table. He looked over the entire crew for a minute then he said, "Well, the first thing I would like to say from the bottom of my heart is thank you. I want to thank the officers and crew of this submarine for all their help. Without you, I'm afraid we would not be alive today. Then I would like to thank the good doctor, who never left Kellie's side till she was out of danger. I feel he really worked a miracle. Thank you all again."

When the applause finally died down, Gordy looked around the mess again slowly, then he began saying, "Like the iceberg and the *Titanic*, we were destined to meet in the Coral Sea, believe it or not. Just as every star in the sky is always exactly in the right spot at the right time, and no mountain is ever in the wrong place, so it is with the hunter and the prey. All things have their place in the plan that the Creator has for us all. There are only challenges and opportunities, no mistakes."

In the blink of an eye, Gordy went back to when he would listen to the stories that Charley would spread out before him, like a picture in an intricate tapestry. So often he could remember his old friend Charley saying, "The telling of the hunt will last long after the taste of the meat has gone." He also remembered Charley talking of really great hunters and brave warriors among his ancestors. Gordy thought, *These great hunters and warriors had done real noble and brave deeds, far beyond anything I have done.*

Gordy didn't really feel like a hero, but he was here. He continued, "I learned to hunt in the deep woods of the great Rocky Mountains. My teacher was an old Indian chief called Charley Greywolf. He was a mighty hunter and the son of a mighty hunter. He taught me how to talk with the animals of the forest and the birds of the sky. Charley taught me how to listen with my spirit as well as my ears. Indeed, he was a great teacher. My friend and teacher Charley had no sons of his own, so he treated me as his son. He taught me all the hunting skills which his father had taught him. Charley had been told by his father that if you don't pass on the hunting skills you are taught, they slowly die. So as it turned out, my friend Charley needed me as much as I needed him. My teacher would often tell me it was all planned by the Great Spirit, that there are no mistakes."

Gordy hesitated for a few minutes, then said, "I injured my left foot badly when my ship was in Rabaul, about four months ago. While in the Rabaul General Hospital, I met this gorgeous little Aussie nurse, Kellie. I had never seen anything quite like Kellie; she knocked me completely for a loop. After being there for three weeks, I was sent to the Sydney General Hospital to recuperate.

"When I was well and could walk again, I tried to find out if Kellie was still in Rabaul. Nobody in Sydney would give me any information. They claimed it was all classified. A soldier I met in a pub one night claimed he had been in Rabaul as recently as two weeks before. He told me nearly all the whites on the island had been brought back to Australia. This soldier claimed if I went to Darwin and talked to this certain army captain, he would be able to assist me. There were at least ten thousand soldiers in Sydney at that particular time. Why I went into that one certain pub and met that one soldier who knew who I needed to contact, is definitely more than a chance coincidence!

"So I went to Darwin and looked up that army captain and he made some phone calls. He found out that Kellie had stayed in Rabaul to help the native girls. While we were talking he remembered his old pilot friend Allan was flying a spotter to Rabaul that very night. The pilot was late taking off that night due to some minor electrical problem. The captain browbeat his old pilot friend into taking one more passenger. 'You're going there anyway, what's one more passenger?' he said.

"There are no mistakes according to my old friend Charley. There are challenges and there are problems. If I had not got on that particular plane that night, I would have arrived in Rabaul too late to be of any use to Kellie."

Gordy stopped to take a swallow of his coffee, then he began again, "The Japanese arrived in Rabaul one day after I walked out of the hospital, with Kellie draped over my shoulder like a side of beef. Kellie was not one bit happy with this kind of treatment, and she was threatening me with all kinds of horrible deaths."

The crew were sitting on the edge of their seats by now and Kellie had a funny little grin on her face. She knew that Gordy was in his glory, telling all these salty characters a yarn the likes of which they had never heard. He again stopped to sip what was left of his coffee, but Kellie knew Gordy was just getting warmed up. She had heard all the stories before, but they still held her speechless and wanting to have it all explained again.

Gordy told them, "Three Japanese soldiers had found the small hut the natives had built for the spotter, and they smashed the radio he was going to use for his operation. Archie, the spotter, had worked on the island of New Britain for over twenty years and he knew most of the natives and their families. A lot of the natives had worked for him for years. Three Japanese soldiers had captured George, one of the spotter's oldest native friends. Archie was much to old to try a rescue operation of this kind, so I volunteered to try and save his old friend."

Gordy lowered his voice, then he started telling them, "I crept along on my belly like an eel, till I got to the exact spot where I could get a shot at the two Japanese soldiers who were guarding George. They had knocked the poor fellow out with a blow on the head with a rifle butt. I carefully shot the first two soldiers high in the chest so they would fall over backwards." Gordy stopped for a minute, as though he was trying to get the events straight in his head.

Then he explained in detail the last soldier's death. "The third soldier, who was inside the hut, waited a long time before he made a move. He was in between a rock and a very hard place. If he made a mistake, his military career would be over and he would join his friends. The poor fellow had only one thing he could do. I knew it, and I'm sure he knew it.

"The soldier had to sneak out of the back of the thatch hut without being seen or heard. Then he had to sneak up on the enemy who had shot his friends. He would loose face if he went back to his base and admitted he had not tried to kill his enemy." Gordy milked the incident of the last soldier's demise for every drop of excitement there was to be had. He told the sub's crew, "The Japanese soldier must have been convinced that the enemy was in a treetop because his two friends had fallen over backwards. They were trained to use that tactic, so he naturally thought the enemy was also trained to do that."

Gordy hesitated a minute then said, "The third soldier hugged the ground like a thin coat of oil, then he would lift his head a little. Not any more than he had to, but enough so that he could look up into the treetops.

"On the fourth or fifth time he raised his head, he put himself right into the sights of my rifle." Gordy then described, "I squeezed the trigger ever so slowly, so as not to spoil my aim. The brave soldier didn't even hear the shot that sent him to join his friends in their idea of heaven." One sailor spilt his cup of coffee in his lap, he was so engrossed in the tale. Not one sailor in the mess had got up and moved. Some of the younger sailors hardly breathed during the whole narration.

Captain Finch suggested they stop and get a fresh cup of coffee before Gordy went on with the story. The captain had never heard the crew so quiet for so long a time. It seemed to him they were always bitching and complaining about something, and this might just make them realize how well they had it.

When they were all sitting down again, the captain apologized to Gordy for the interruption, and asked him if he would please continue. Gordy looked over at Kellie again and she had a little grin on her face, so he knew it was all right to go on. She was sitting next to the captain and it looked funny with her in an ordinary sailor's suit, he in all his gold braid.

Gordy said, "When George and I had disposed of the three soldiers in a ravine, we knew it would be dangerous to stay around there. More Japanese soldiers were bound to show up sooner or later. We agreed that we might as well move to the small native village after Archie's radio was all smashed to pieces. George, the native friend who had been captured by the Japanese, went with his wife to her village to get a large catamaran for us to sail back to Australia in. The first day George was away, five Japanese soldiers arrived at the village in a small landing craft. The Japanese rounded up all of the villagers and had them huddled in the middle of the village compound.

"The idea was to take them to some other part of the island, probably to work on some project they were constructing. They apparently move the families to the site and then the workers will stay there. We knew that the native friend of Archie's would not be too happy if he came back and found his family had been taken away. We had to do something to try and help the people of the village. They were friendly, beautiful people and didn't deserve being shoved around by the Japanese."

Gordy hesitated a minute. He looked slowly around the mess and saw everyone was waiting to hear what happened. "My friend Archie, the would-be spotter, and I made out way down to the village on our bellies. Then Archie, who was a tough little skinny character, crawled around the entire village on his belly. He then fastened a piece of thin copper wire from a radio coil, onto a long slender branch of a large bush, on the far side of the village. When Archie finally got back nearly an hour later, he was drenched in sweat but he had done the job. I put a full clip into the rifle and aimed at one of the soldiers closest to us. I waited a few minutes to give Archie time to get his breath. It was extremely hot that day, and I could hear Archie huffing and puffing like a locomotive.

"When I gave the signal, Archie pulled on the thin copper wire. One of the Japanese soldiers thought there was someone behind the bush. He yelled some order in Japanese and raised his rifle. I told Archie to make the branch move again. The soldier fired at the bush and I fired at the same time. When one of the soldiers fell over; that made the rest of them think they were being attacked. They all started to fire at the bush at the same time, and I picked them off one after the other. The soldiers didn't even tumble to the oldest trick in the book. Hunters of all countries have been using the moving branch trick for as long as there have been hunters. The cave men of prehistoric times used the same method, in hunting saber-toothed tigers.

"That night, Archie was the hero of the village. The people of the village had known and worked for Archie for many years. He was always fair and easy to get along with, so the natives all respected the little wiry character. It was probably the first time in his long life that Archie was looked up to as a real honest-to-God hero. Sad to say, the new status of hero was to be short lived."

Then Gordy hesitated for a minute. He said, "A small navy launch with about thirty Imperial Marines on board arrived at the village early the following morning. With all the excitement of the previous day, everyone in the village had overslept that morning. The Imperial Marines caught poor Archie before he had time to get away. The tough little character kicked one of the marines right off the jetty, and for that little bravado, he was clubbed over the head with a rifle butt. Archie was then picked up like a sack of potatoes and thrown onto the launch. There was nothing we could do against that many of them, after all, we only had one rifle." Gordy shook his head, like he was trying hard not to think of something very disagreeable.

"The following day, Archie's native friend George arrived back with the large ceremonial catamaran from his wife's village. The natives of George's village scrounged their larders to fill every nook and cranny of the canoe with food. The kindness and generosity of these beautiful people is really amazing. George told me how to navigate by the sun and stars. He told me I had to find this certain tiny atoll and hide there on the first day, or the Japanese would certainly find us. We were sailing at night and were lucky to find such a small dot on such a large ocean."

After a moment's pause, Gordy said, "We found the small atoll and took the sail off the canoe so it wouldn't be spotted. We used the sail as a mattress and went to sleep in no time at all. I had not closed my eyes all night and was dead tired. Kellie woke up in four and a half hours. When she looked around, she almost died of fright. She grabbed me and shouted for me to wake up. A mile away from the atoll was the largest ship I have ever seen in my life. I swear this ship must have been one of the largest battleships in the world, and to make matters worse, its sixteen-inch guns were pointing right at the little atoll. Looking at those huge gun barrels sent a shiver right through both of us.

"Then what looked like a new Japanese destroyer cut between the atoll and the battleship. It too was an impressive ship. I'd swear this sleek-looking vessel was making over forty knots. After settling down a bit, we scoured the little atoll for food, but there was not a scrap we could add to our larder.

81

We had a cup of water and a piece of fruit for lunch. Then Kellie spotted a big turtle trying to get up on the beach. The turtle looked like it may have been injured by the propellers of the speedy destroyer. One of its back legs had been completely severed."

Gordy smiled when he told them, "Kellie was very upset when I killed the damaged turtle and cooked it. If you can imagine it, the meat tasted like an old rubber gum-boot. The first time Kellie tried to eat some of it, she threw up. But after a couple of weeks with very little food, I think her taste buds died and she was able to swallow the terrible stuff. Believe it or not, I'm convinced it was the meat from that three-legged turtle, which kept us alive till we were picked up by the *Croydon*."

Gordy stopped talking for a minute while he drained his coffee cup. Then he continued, "The intense heat beating down on us every day nearly drove us stark raving mad. We tried not to think or talk about the day when the food and water would be gone. The putrid water ran out three days before we were finally picked up. We just sailed on and on, knowing that we were dying a little more each day. I thought for sure our brains would actually get fried by the blasted sun. By the calendar we were only about thirty-four days and nights in the boat, but by now it seemed like we had been afloat for months. Not one thing alive did we see, just waves and more endless bloody waves."

Gordy looked over and saw Kellie was getting tired, so he thought it was time to shut down the show for the night. He hesitated for a minute then said, "Well once more I am going to thank you, on behalf of Kellie and myself. As you can see, the little lady is nodding her head, so it is time we hit the bunks." The crew stood and gave the young couple another standing ovation.

They were both touched by the attention they had received that night. Then to add to the excitement, Captain Finch got up and presented Gordy and Kellie with a plaque with the insignia of the H.M.S. *Croydon* on it. Gordy almost broke down.

When the presentation was over, the crew swarmed around and asked them questions for the next ten or fifteen minutes. One of the men asked Kellie if they were going to get married when they got home. Kellie thought for a minute, then said, "We will have to get married now, or my dad will kill us both." They all laughed.

Kellie and Gordy made their way back to the cabin they were using, and Kellie climbed into her bunk first. She was very quiet for a few minutes, then she said, "Gordy, I hope you are never sorry that you came back to Rabaul for me."

Gordy looked over at Kellie. He smiled and went over to her, "You never need to worry your head about that, little one. I'm sure we were brought together by divine appointment. Like the bird and the song or the bee and the flower, believe me, we are a pair. So go to sleep now and in one more day we will be back safe and sound, in good old Aussie." Kellie went to sleep that night feeling more wanted and loved than she had ever felt in her whole life.

Gordy sat on the side of his bunk for a while and he looked over at Kellie, all snuggled up in her bunk. He hadn't told her. When the *Croydon* appeared just behind their catamaran, he had picked up the rifle by the barrel and was going to bash her brains in. In his fuddled mental state, he was sure it was a Japanese submarine that had found them. The swell from the sub's hull nearly tipped them over, and he lost the rifle when he grabbed hold of the mast. The great rescue had nearly ended in a greater tragedy.

The cook was quite often admonished by the captain when too much food was thrown overboard, but since the big Canadian was eating regularly, nothing went over the side. Gordy was always the last to leave the table and he never forgot to thank the cook at least three times. On the last morning the cook put on a feast; he wanted to use up a lot of the old stores, so there was double of everything.

Captain Finch invited Gordy and Kellie up to the bridge for the last few hours before were to tie up. Gordy was still devouring whatever was left over after the crew had finished eating. On the bridge with Captain Finch were the first mate and two seamen lookouts. When Kellie came up to the bridge, in the sailor rig, the captain said, "This is Mr. Corbit, my first officer. It is his cabin that you have been using." Kellie shook hands and thanked him very much for letting them use his cabin.

Mr. Corbit said, "It was a great pleasure for me to be of help." When Kellie finally got her hand away from him, she turned again to say something to the captain. The mate then made a suggestive sign to the two crew members about Kellie's slim little figure.

Just at that opportune moment, Gordy stuck his head through the hatch. The mate was about to swing into action and he adjusted his cap, so that a few of his black curls fell down over his forehead. Gordy came onto the bridge then, and the captain, with a smile on his face, said, "Mr. Cameron, I would like to introduce you to my first mate, Mr. Corbit." Gordy, being a sailor himself, could read this son of a sea cook like a book. He knew exactly what the moron had in mind.

When the first mate put out his hand, Gordy grabbed it and squeezed very hard. He kept squeezing until he could see the pain in the mate's eyes. Then something gave way in the mate's hand, so Gordy let go. Mr. Corbit suddenly looked very pale and shaky. He asked for permission to leave the bridge, and the captain waved his permission. When the first mate had gone below, the captain burst out laughing and said, "That crazy mate of mine has even had the nerve to make a pass at my dear wife. My wife is old enough to be his blasted mother."

The captain laughed again. Even the two crew members thought it was real funny. They didn't like the mate at any time. The first mate definitely was not the most popular member of the crew. When Mr. Corbit went below, he went to the doctor's cabin and told him he had hurt his hand coming down the ladder from the bridge. The second mate came up onto the bridge in a few minutes and asked, "What happened to the mate? Corbit claimed that he hurt his hand coming down the ladder. Is that right?" Captain Finch told the second mate what really happened and they both had a laugh over it.

The captain formally introduced Gordy and Kellie to Tom Burns, his second mate. Tom said, "By the way, where are you going after we get to Freemantle?"

Kellie said, "We are going to my parent's place at St. Kilda, in Melbourne. They don't have a clue what has become of me and will be worried sick. I will have to phone them as soon as we get ashore. My parents are going to have a ruddy fit when I tell them what had happened in the last month."

The second mate thought for a minute, then he said, "How would you and your friend like to ride to Melbourne with me? I'd love the company, to tell you the truth. I have a month's leave coming to me, so I'm going home to see my family. I have a fairly large car and maybe we can take turns driving. It is one long drive for someone on their own, believe me I would really appreciate the company. We could get there early on the fifth day, or maybe even very late on the fourth day if we really hump it."

The second mate waited to let Kellie and Gordy think the proposition over. Then Tom said, "I have been saving gas-ration coupons for six months and my family has mailed me some of theirs, so I have just enough to make it there and back. The only problem is, I won't be leaving till early tomorrow morning, but you would sure be welcome to come along if you want. Talk it over, and let me know later."

Captain Finch had been listening to them talk and he said, "What a smashing idea! You young people can come home with me for the night, and Tom can pick you up at my place in the morning. My dear wife Helen is a real romantic, and if I let you go without her meeting you she would never give me a moment's peace, so help me."

Kellie looked at the captain and said, "Your wife has not seen you for a long time. Are you sure it would be all right with Missus Finch? You have done so much for us already, we shouldn't impose on you any longer."

Captain Finch smiled at Kellie, standing there in her sailor suit and said, "Nonsense, Kellie. You and Gordon have made this trip the most exciting voyage of the war, so far. We are told by the navy brass to patrol a certain area of a very large ocean. Most of the time it is so boring. I wish the crew would mutiny just for some excitement. You two have given us all something to talk about for a long time to come. My dear wife and I live alone now. One son is with the army in North Africa someplace. The other son is in medical school and he only gets home every six months." The captain hesitated a moment then said, "My good wife Helen loves visitors, and if I didn't bring you two home so she could meet both of you, she will shoot me. When I am away at sea she is busy with her volunteer work with other navy wives, but she really loves young people. So please say you will come and stay with us till morning."

When the submarine got to Freemantle, they sailed along the docks where submarines were lined up in long rows. The *Croydon* was finally tied up to the right berth. Then the captain took Gordy and Kellie to the officer's club for a couple of drinks. The captain left them to phone his wife, and he told her about the two young visitors who would be staying the night. When they all arrived at the captain's house, his wife Helen was waiting at the front door for them. They all followed her into the beautiful front room of the red brick house. Kellie still had the sailor suit on and she looked like such a character. The captain's wife had a big smile on her face as she looked at Kellie.

After the captain made the introductions, she insisted that they call her Helen, and she could call them Kellie and Gordon. Helen looked at the young couple and said, "You two look like you need a good hot cup of tea and some muffins." With that Helen left for the kitchen and they heard the water running and then the quietness.

Captain Finch said in a hushed voice, "Helen will be weeping as she makes the tea. I've never seen such a softhearted person in my life. But to tell you the truth, I wouldn't want her any other way." Sure enough, when Helen came back they could see that she had been weeping. She set the tea tray down on a small table and came over to Kellie, and gave her a big hug.

Finally Helen said, "Tell me, Gordon, is it true that you went back to Rabaul to rescue Kellie, even though you knew that the Japanese were coming?" Gordy didn't know what to say. He didn't want to appear as a show off and a braggart in front of this nice lady. He could easily see that she was a tenderhearted soul, the kind of lady who lives for good music, fine paintings, and tender love stories.

"Well you see, Helen, it is like this," Gordon said, "I have a very old dear aunt in Vancouver, and she loves to read people's tea leaves. She read mine once, and she told me that I would be badly injured in a faraway port. My dear old aunt said that the first woman I would see when I woke up would be the one I would spend my life with. And amazing as it sounds, she was right. My ship was in Rabaul and I was injured. I woke up the next day in the hospital, and the first person I saw when I woke up was Kellie. So you see, I really had no choice. It as written in the tea leaves that I would go back to Rabaul. When I saw those great big brown eyes in that pretty little face, I thought I had already died and gone to heaven."

Helen gave Kellie another big hug, then she came over and hugged Gordy. Tears were rolling down her face and she said, "That is the most beautiful thing I have ever heard." Kellie was now weeping too, so Helen went to her and the two of them hugged again and cried.

The captain said, "Come on you two characters, break it up! Kellie should go now and phone up her folks in Melbourne." They all had a big laugh at the waterworks display. The captain said, "You know, when I first met Helen she would cry at the drop of a hat, so help me. I was beginning to think her eyes were hooked up to her kidneys for a while." They all laughed again.

Helen said, "Henry's right, Kellie, why don't you go into the other room and phone your folks right now. Then when you come back we can all have another cup of hot tea. I swear you two have been through so much and they will be worried sick."

Kellie was going to ask Gordy to come with her but she didn't. She got up slowly and walked into the other room. She suddenly wasn't sure what she would say to her parents. She felt almost scared to phone them up. Her dad thought she was bonkers for staying in Rabaul, when all the white people were leaving. It took Kellie a good five minutes to get her composure back, and then she dialed her parents' phone number. A minute later, she heard the phone ring.

Kellie's mother answered the phone, and said, "Hello, who is speaking please?" Kellie said, "Mom, it's me, Kellie." She heard a thud like someone falling on the floor, then no one said anything. She knew if she waited long enough someone would come to the phone, or her mother would finally wake up.

A few minutes went by, then her father came on the phone and shouted, "Who the hell is this?" Kellie said, "It's me, Dad, it's Kellie! I'm in Freemantle right now, and I should be home in four or five days at the most. A great big Canadian bloke came and rescued me from Rabaul. We are going to get married I think; tell Mom not to bust her boiler, will you?"

Her dad shouted, "Hold on a minute there girl, what the ruddy hell do you mean you're getting hitched? What is this ruddy bloke like? Is he coming here with you? Blimey, you sure are a beaut, that's all I can say! Your poor mom and me didn't even know for sure if you were still alive, then you suddenly phone up and say you're getting hitched. You should have told us sooner, girl."

"Dad, listen to me. We were out in the middle of the ruddy ocean and were rescued by a blinking submarine. We were almost dead. If it weren't for Gordy, I would be dead right now, believe me! Now listen. I will phone again in a day or two and tell you where we are. Love you all," then she hung up.

Kellie almost had to laugh; her dad always yelled when he talked on the phone. He never could get the idea in his head that you don't have to yell when you are talking on the phone. It was so good to hear her dad again; he was such a character.

For a while, Kellie just sat by the phone and tried to picture what was going on in her parents' house right now. Her dad would open up a beer first thing. Then he would yell for his old cobber, Bluey, who lived two doors down the street. Then Bluey would come over for a cold one. And her mom would be on the phone, calling her older sister, Donna. The place would be buzzing, that would be for sure. Between phone calls her mom would be going into the kitchen, making a cup of tea, and having a weep. Then her mother would be back on the phone to all her friends, talking a hundred miles and hour.

Her dad would sit with Bluey, telling him the news. Then they would stroll down to the pub to tell the rest of his mates. A couple of hours later he would come home and sit in his chair with another cold one. He was proud of his daughter; she had worked so hard to get to be a first-class nurse.

Kellie went back into the other room and they had another cup of tea and some scones. She sat close to Gordy and thought, *My dad is going to like this bloke, that's for sure. He will want to drag Gordy down to the pub whenever he can, to meet his mates.* And when it comes to telling yarns, she knew Gordy could hold his own. Some of her dad's mates told some of the dumbest stories she ever heard. Kellie was sure they never happened, but it didn't seem to matter to anyone.

Helen cooked up a beautiful leg-of-lamb dinner and Kellie and Gordy enjoyed every little morsel. The sub's cook was pretty good, but not in the same league as Helen. Before they turned in for the night, Kellie and Gordy wanted to go for a short walk. It felt odd being on dry land again, knowing they were safe at last. Living on the edge of death for a long period of time had left them exhausted. They slowly walked around a little tree-filled park near the captain's house. They were holding hands and relaxing in the warm, friendly land breeze. Each step they took was almost intoxicating.

Kellie would look up at Gordy every few minutes and wonder what it was going to be like married to this big bloke. As if he had been reading her mind, Gordy said, "By the way, little one, I never did ask you if you wanted to marry me. Just because I came back and helped you get out of Rabaul, does not mean that you have to marry me."

Kellie looked up at him and smiled, "You don't think for a minute that I'm going to make a liar out of your little old aunt in Vancouver, do you? You are not trying to wiggle out of it, are you, Gordon? It is just not that easy to do, Mr. Gordon Cameron. I told my dad that you dragged me away from my job and he said you have to support me now, so there." They both laughed as they walked back to the captain's house.

"Tell me something, will you, Gordon? I know that you have been a sailor and have probably been with a lot of girls. Why didn't you ever try to have your way with me?" asked Kellie.

Gordy hesitated a moment before he answered; he knew this answer could mean a lot of trouble down the road if it came out wrong. "Well little one, I thought about it on more than one occasion, believe me." Gordy hesitated again, then he said, "I wanted to be able to look your family in the eye when I met them. Not only that, I have to look myself in the eye every day, no exceptions. I was told years ago by my old friend Charley, that the arrow that is the straightest goes the farthest. Another friend I met one time told me that if you don't stand for something you will fall for anything. So, little one, I hope I have answered your question." Kellie didn't say any more.

When they got back to the captain's house they both turned in, and exhaustion settled over them like a mist once more. At seven o'clock the next morning, the second mate, Tom Burns, arrived in his Old Rover. Helen got up and made a great breakfast. After a few tearful goodbyes, they climbed into Tom's station wagon. Although it was six years old, the car was still in perfect condition because it was in storage for the bigger part of the year. There was even a thick blanket in the back so someone could snooze in the back while the others drove.

Gordy asked Tom, "Do you think we could swing by the dock, so we can take a look at the *Croydon* one more time? You know Tom, I already have a hard time believing it all really happened." They stopped at the dock for a good ten minutes and took a good look at the submarine that had saved their lives. Tom didn't say a word, he just sat and waited. Kellie had the weirdest feeling in her stomach as she looked at the submarine. Then she looked at Gordy and realized he was feeling the very same emotions, thinking how close they had come to dying in the Coral Sea.

Chapter Eleven

WELCOME HOME

As they were driving away from the dock area, Gordy knew he would never be able to take life for granted again. His outlook on things had been altered forever. They took turns driving and covered many miles that first day. Gordy had to keep his wits about him as he drove; all the driving he had ever done was on the other side of the road. Tom had brought two large Thermos bottles full of tea and a big box of sandwiches, so the first day they didn't have to stop once. At ten o'clock the following morning, they stopped for breakfast. They took a short brisk walk around a soccer pitch, then off they went again.

The road closely followed the coastline and was very dangerous, especially at night. A driver could easily fall asleep and go off the road. He could wind up in the surf in no time flat. The small communities along the coast road were few and far between. Tom had to make sure he filled the tank up with petrol, before the stations closed down at night. Once the petrol stations closed, the operators would go home.

Most times they stopped to fill up with petrol, they had a cup of tea and one or two meat pies. One of the truck stops had a pub, and it was very popular with the long-distance truckers. Tom decided to stop there and have a cold one, and top up the petrol tank. Gordy was having a doze in the back of the car. He had decided to bypass the refreshments this time, as he was bushed. Tom went into the pub and got two cold ones for Kellie and himself. Kellie had chosen to sit at a table on the pub's veranda and when Tom got back with the beers, there were two tough-looking truckers with her. Tom said, "If you blokes want a beer, you will have to go inside and get your own."

The bigger and tougher-looking character said, "Buzz off, mate! Can't you ruddy well see we are having a little visit with our lady friend?" Tom didn't know exactly what to do for a minute. He knew he couldn't beat both of these morons, and they looked like they just wanted him to start something.

These two miserable-looking characters were up to no good, so he said, "The young lady had another friend in the car. You might want to meet this bloke; he likes to meet all her new friends." Tom walked over to the car and shook Gordon a bit. He said, "Kellie has a couple of friends she would like you to meet, Gordy." When he woke up and climbed out of the car, Tom had a grin on his face. He remembered what happened to the first mate when he got cute with Kellie. Gordy walked slowly over to the veranda. He looked like he was half asleep as he walked and he pretended to yawn, but he was really looking the two thugs over carefully, deciding on his way to the veranda, that the only threat came from the bigger ape.

Gordy reached the veranda and ambled slowly over to the table and said, "I'm a friend of the young lady. My name is Gordon, what is yours?" He put out his hand as if it shake hands with the trucker. The big ape told Gordy, "Bugger off." Gordy grabbed his hand so quick the large trucker didn't realize what happened. The gorilla clenched his other hand and was going to swing at Gordy, but the hand Gordy had was in his grip like a steel vice. He closed on the man's fingers till a distinct snap could be heard. It was evident that something had broken. The ugly look on the moron's face spelled out plainly the pain he was in. The trucker banged on the table, so Gordy let go of his hand. Then he leaned over the table, and said, "If I was you, squirt, I would help your mate to a doctor." The two toughs took off down the road in a hurry, the big one moaning in agony.

"Well, now that I'm fully awake I might as well have a cold one myself," said Gordy. Tom went inside and got Gordy a glass of beer. When he came back out, he said, "Kellie, I really don't think that your friends like your boyfriend at all." They all roared with laughter. Once more they took a quick sprint around the little community, then they climbed back into the Rover and continued their journey. All day they followed the coast, and the scenery was beyond anything Gordy had ever seen. Gorgeous beaches for miles on end, every time they turned around one headland, there would be another great expanse of white sandy beach. The backdrop of dark blue water made the white sand looked even whiter. Tom did most of the driving in the daytime because Gordy would always be glancing at the scenery as he drove. He nearly ran off the road two or three times.

They made good time at night, each one of them taking turns driving for no more than two hours at a time. They drove all night, and the next morning they had breakfast in the small town of Esperance. They had steak and eggs for breakfast that morning and Gordy thought, *That is more like a real breakfast.* They gassed up again and took the show on the road once more. The weather had cooled down a bit and the driving was a lot easier. You wouldn't stick to the leather seats any more, so you didn't have to keep squirming around all the time.

After refueling in Ukla, they drove right through to Wyalla. It was a beautiful spot, so they bought some meat pies and soft drinks. Then they stretched out on a nice grassy patch in a small park and rested for two hours. It was so refreshing! They had another picnic in a small park in Spencer Gulf. The next day they reached Adelaide, where Kellie phoned her folks again. She told them that they would be in Melbourne late the following day. Kellie talked to her mom and told her not to go to any trouble for them, although she knew her mom would want everything just so. Her dad came on the phone again and Kellie warned him, "Be careful, Dad, when you shake hands with Gordy; he's very strong."

It was ten-thirty the next night, by the time they got to the place where Tom had promised to drop them off. Gordy was actually glad to get out of the car. He had never imagined the drive would be that far. Once more they thanked Tom profusely for all his help. They both had to agree that he was one bonzer bloke, as Kellie put it.

Kellie then phoned her dad. She told him where they were, and also said they would have to take a taxi home. "Neither of us have money with us, so can you pay the taxi?" she asked. Her dad yelled into the phone, "I will be waiting on the porch love, so stop talking, girl, and get over here!" Forty minutes later, the taxi pulled up in front of a red brick house with all the lights on. Kellie's dad came out and paid the driver. He then grabbed Kellie and gave her a big long hug. When he eventually looked over her shoulder he saw the young man standing there.

Her dad said, "I take it this must be Gordy. My name is Jim, and I am ever glad to meet you, young man! You are more than welcome in this house, Gordon. From what I hear from the girl, we owe you a great deal, mate."

Jim then said to Gordy, "We tried our best to talk Kellie out of staying in Rabaul, but she is as pig-headed as her old dad. When we heard the news that the Nips had landed in Rabaul, we nearly died, I'll tell you. She is a bonzer little nurse and we are proud of her. I only wish she would use her head a little more, fair dinkum."

Kellie urged them to go inside, "Mom is waiting for us, Dad, and she will have a fit if we stay out here any longer."

"You're absolutely right, love. Let's go inside, Gordon, and meet the rest of the mob," said Jim. When they entered the front door, Kellie's mom grabbed Kellie and gave her a long motherly hug. Hesitantly, she put her hand out to Gordy. "Mom, he won't hurt you, really," said Kellie reaching up and giving Gordy a big kiss. Everybody laughed. Then Kellie's mom gave Gordy a big motherly hug too, and said, "Thank you, son, for helping our Kellie get home safely."

Gordy was kind of flabbergasted. He did not know what to say. He thought for a minute then he said, "Kellie is a great nurse, one of the best I imagine, and an exceptionally fine person also. When I found out that Kellie was still in Rabaul, and the Japanese were going to land there any day. I just had to go back and see if I could help her. I'm sure lots of people would have been glad to go and help Kellie, if they had known where she was. But I'm glad it was me who found her first. And if you have no objections, I would like to marry Kellie. I promise I will look after her and make sure no harm comes to her." There was a sudden funny feeling in the room; they more or less knew that Kellie and Gordon would get married later on, but this was a little sudden. After all, they had just met this big Canadian bloke twenty minutes ago, now he announced that he wanted to marry their youngest daughter. Kellie's mom looked over at the dad to say something.

Jim stood up and his voice shook with emotion, "It is we who are honored, young man, believe me. Not many blokes I know would have done what you have done, risking your life for someone you hardly know. A lot of blokes might do it for someone they have known for years, but not for someone they hardly know." Jim paused for a minute then looked at Kellie, "Well Kellie girl, are you going to marry this bloke or are you going to drive him bonkers trying to figure out the answer?"

All eyes turned to Kellie. She had been sitting with her mom on the sofa and she got up and walked over to the chair where Gordy sat. She said, "The doctor who looked after us on the submarine told me that if Gordy had not kept me from drifting into comas all the time, I would have wound up a vegetable. I would not have wanted that. The many weeks we spent in the canoe are mostly a blur. I know if Gordy had not looked after me, I would have fallen overboard a few times." She almost broke into tears. Then Kellie said, "And that ruddy turtle meat he made me eat. I know it probably saved my life. It made me sick as a dog when I first tried to eat it, but later when I could no longer taste anything, Gordy would keep stuffing that revolting stuff down my throat."

Kellie paused again. "When he walked into the hospital and threw me over his shoulder like a side of beef, I'm so glad I didn't know what was ahead of us. Gordy risked his own life to get me off the island and I'm sure I would be dead now if he hadn't. Of course I will be happy to marry you, Gordon Cameron, if you still want me."

Kellie's poor mom had tears rolling down her face, looking from Kellie to Gordy, then back again to Kellie.

Finally Jim said, "I don't know if anyone knows it or not, but it's two o'clock in the ruddy morning and these people must be bushed. I know I am. This had been a great day for our family, so let's hit the bunks now and do a lot more talking tomorrow." And so the day that was so long in arriving finally came to a perfect end. Exhaustion crept over the whole family, and they went to sleep knowing that their most precious prayers had been answered in full.

The next two weeks were wild and hectic, what with the plans for the wedding in full swing. Everything was put on hold for the wedding and the whole family, from almost every state in Australia, was going to be represented. Kellie took Gordy around to meet all the nursing friends she had trained with. When they had heard that Gordy had gone back to rescue Kellie from Rabaul, they thought it was all so romantic and they envied her. When Kellie told then how Gordy had thrown her over his shoulder like a side of beef and walked out of the hospital with her, they thought it was priceless.

Twice Kellie's dad dragged Gordy down to the pub to meet his mates. Jim would tell them of the exploits that Gordy had gone through to rescue his Kellie, and then the beer would be on the house. Because Jim drank most of it, Gordy had to help him home both nights. A lot of Jim's mates were old army types and they loved the stories.

Kellie's older sister Donna was married to Walter, who was a freelance reporter on one of the big newspapers in Melbourne. Walter wanted to write a story for the paper about Gordy and Kellie's harrowing escape from Rabaul. After he had finished the story, he showed it to Gordy. Walter made it read like a movie script, and Gordy thought he had overdone it a bit. Walter had to admit that he had got carried away just a little, so he agreed to tell it just the way it happened. The story was printed on the front page, and it still made Gordy look like a big hero. Gordy bought a couple copies and sent them home, one to his dear old aunt and one to his dad. Gordy knew that his dad would spread it all over town and his dear old aunt would tell all her old girlfriends. It would give them both enough to talk about until he and Kellie got there for a visit.

Two days before the wedding was to take place, the phone rang and there was someone on the line who wanted to talk to Gordy. When he went to the phone, the person on the other end said, "Thank God, you made it, Canada. This is Captain Denny, and I thought I had sent you on a one-way ticket, fair dinkum. That night you took off in the plane to Rabaul, I really kicked myself for getting involved. When I thought it over, I didn't think you had a chance in hell of ever coming back."

Gordy could hear the captain hesitate a couple of times, then he said, "You see, I didn't know if you even got to Rabaul or not, till I read that great story in the paper yesterday. I don't suppose you know; the plane and pilot never made it back to Darwin. What happened to my old cobber, Allan, no one knows. I read the story over about three times before I was really sure it was you. I'm ruddy well glad you made it, mate. Can we meet for lunch today, Gordon? I would love to see you again and bring that little beaut in the picture with you." The captain told Gordy what hotel he was staying in, and they arranged to meet at two o'clock for lunch.

Gordy and Kellie arrived at the hotel early. Gordy had time to tell Kellie how the captain had made arrangements for him to fly to Rabaul with an old mate of his. Gordy said, "If the captain had not gone out of his way to help me, I would not have got to Rabaul for another two or three weeks at least. It would not have been a wedding we would be celebrating on Saturday, I assure you. He's one great guy, believe me."

The captain turned up at two and they had a great lunch. The captain thought Kellie was a real prize. He said, "You didn't tell me she was this beautiful Gordon, or I would have taken the flight myself and left you in Darwin." They had a chuckle at the captain's sly compliment to Kellie's beauty. Gordy told the captain about the spotter, Archie MacCauly, and how he had been taken away by the Japanese marines. He told the captain that they would have been taken prisoner too, if they had tried to rescue him. There was just nothing they could do. It was a tough call to make, and the captain agreed.

Captain Denny was sorry he wouldn't be able to be at the wedding. He was scheduled to leave for Darwin the following morning. He told Gordy, "This has been the best day of my whole leave. I really felt that I had sent you to meet your maker, Gordy, and it bothered the hell out of me. Many nights I thought, I should not try to help every sad mother's son that comes along. You'll never know how relieved I am, fair dinkum." Captain Denny wished them a long happy life, then they parted. Kellie had never thought to ask Gordy how he got to Rabaul, and she was amazed how things had worked out.

The great wedding day finally arrived and Kellie's parents were so happy for their youngest daughter. It turned out to be a perfect day. The myriad of birds were singing like a choir and the flowers were at their most fragrant. Kellie looked like she had just stepped out of a high-class book advertising beautiful wedding gowns. It truly was a magnificent day and only one thing in the whole world could have made it any better: having his dad there, along with his old friends, Charley and Vera.

After the greatest wedding Gordy and Kellie had ever seen, they went to Apollo Bay for their two-week honeymoon. The drive up the ocean highway was breathtaking, with miles and miles of the most fantastic beaches and scenery that one can imagine. Apollo Bay looks over a great expanse of the Indian Ocean, and they would sit on the veranda in the evening drinking tea, thinking how lucky they were. The two weeks' honeymoon went by far too fast. Before they knew it, the honeymoon was almost over. Just before they were to come home, a story in a local paper shook Kellie up terribly. It was a reprint from a story in the main Sydney paper.

The report said, "A spotter on one of the islands up north had sent a radio message, claiming that some natives had seen a dozen drunken Japanese soldiers shoot eight Aussie nurses." They had apparently taken the nurses down to a beach and made them walk into the water then they shot them all, and just left them there. For the rest of that day, Kellie held onto Gordy's arm. Twice she broke into sobs and couldn't stop for nearly half an hour. There was just nothing Gordy could say to cheer her up, so he kept very quiet and let her got through her grief. Kellie cried herself to sleep that night. When she finally slipped into a deep sleep, Gordy got up and went out onto the veranda. The gruesome story in the paper had also bothered him.

When the honeymoon was over they drove home slowly, stopping along the way just to enjoy the view. They would stroll along some of the many magnificent beaches, shared only by the great flocks of sea birds. A week after they got back to Melbourne, Gordy booked passage to Canada on a Swedish ship. The week was busy. They didn't realize how many things there was to do, and the goodbye parties they had to attend.

The day they boarded ship to sail to Canada was a day of tears and of promises to come back soon. Kellie didn't know if she was doing the right thing or not, and when she wasn't laughing, she was crying. Gordy almost felt like letting the lines on the ship go himself, in order to get under way. He thought for sure that Kellie was going to change her mind at any tick of the clock. She was driving them all nuts, and Gordy kept assuring her that they would be back in no time.

At last they dropped the lines and the ship left the dock. Kellie's family were all waving like mad as the ship got farther from the wharf. Soon they were all left behind and Kellie and Gordy kept watching as the land disappeared from view. The first few nights they stayed on deck till it was time to turn in. They just sat snuggled up together watching the stars. It was a fantastic show. The first part of the voyage was perfect. The food was excellent and the time went by at a leisurely pace. The weather was calm and the nights on deck were hypnotic. Many times Kellie would say, "I can see now why you like being a sailor." The warm sea breezes and the sunny days made everything perfect.

In three weeks they reached the Hawaiian islands. The ship stayed in Honolulu for twenty-four hours to refuel and replenish the stores. Gordy and Kellie spent half the day walking around the city. After a good lunch onboard ship, they went to one of the beaches for a swim and a bit of sightseeing. That night they attended one of the night clubs and watched the entertainment. It had been a good day and they were dead tired.

When they awoke in the morning, the ship was already underway. They were only one day from Hawaii when they could feel the change in the temperature. Gradually it became a bit windier. You had to hold onto your hat if you went out on deck. On the third day the wind picked up, and for ten solid days it blew near hurricane force. Kellie got violently seasick and was in bed for the next eight days. She would say to Gordy ten times every day, "Why anyone would be a sailor? I ruddy well can't figure it out." Kellie couldn't eat enough to keep a canary alive. Sometimes Gordy was the only passenger in the dining room.

The storm blew itself out the day before the ship got to Canada. Poor Kellie and the other passengers who had been seasick were, by that time, a pasty-faced lot. Gordy took Kellie for a walk around the deck, and it was so cold Kellie was sure she would freeze her buns off. The snow-capped mountains she had to admit, looked spectacular. But they looked for too cold for her liking.

The next morning, they sailed under the Lions Gate Bridge into Vancouver Harbour and after a big breakfast, they cleared the immigration and customs people. After they got their luggage all sorted out, Gordy phone his dear old aunt.

When Gordy was a little kid of four and five, he used to stay with his aunt and uncle for months at a time. They just loved this little guy and they spoiled him rotten. Then when he went back to his dad, Ed would swear that he would never let Gordy stay with them again, but he always let him go back. Hazel wrote to her brother Ed every couple weeks and she collected a whole scrapbook of pictures of Gordy. Ed never told Hazel when Gordy got in trouble, or anything like that. Hazel was convinced that Gordy was perfect and no one could have told her any different.

Chapter Twelve

The Aunt

When Gordy phoned his dear old aunt, she insisted that they come right over to her apartment. She was so glad that Gordy and his bride had finally arrived. His aunt said, "Gordy, I can't wait to meet Kellie. Tell me, what is she like?"

Gordy laughed and said, "Well to tell you the truth, she looks like a cross between a kangaroo and a koala bear. I really thought they were going to put her into quarantine with the other wild animals. I had to talk like mad with the customs officials, but I finally convinced them she was quite normal for an Australian. They said I could take her with me, if I keep her on a leash." Gordy told his aunt, "We will take a taxi over and be there in half an hour."

When they got to his aunt's apartment, Gordy knocked on the door and hid Kellie behind him. His dear old Aunt Hazel, opened the door and only saw Gordy. "Where is your little lady, Gordy? I thought you would bring her with you."

Gordy looked sad, and said, "Well, when they tested Kellie, they found that she had foot and mouth disease after all so they had to lock her up." Kellie said, "Here I am, Aunty. This big bozo thought it would be funny if he hid me. This bozo has one funny sense of humor, fair dinkum."

"Well Kellie, you should give this big bozo a cuff on the ear for doing such a thing," said Gordy's aunt. "Come over here Kellie, where I can see you better." Gordy's aunt looked Kellie over, then she said, "Gordy, she's a real beauty and I can see now why you went back for her. By the way, Kellie, my name is Hazel, and I hope we are going to be real good friends. When I got the paper from Gordy with the story in it, I got out my atlas and looked up the Coral Sea. It covers about a million miles of tropical ocean. It's really a miracle that you were ever picked up."

Hazel got her atlas for Kellie, and she showed Hazel where it all started, then she showed her approximately where they were finally picked up by the British submarine. After Aunt Hazel made them a nice cup of tea and heated up some scones for them, Gordy then phoned his dad. He talked to him for half an hour, promising that they would be there in a couple of days. Gordy also asked his dad if he would talk to his friend Charley, and ask him of he could take them out into the woods for a couple of days.

That night, Gordy took Kellie and Hazel out to dinner in a real nice restaurant. They had a wonderful time, and Hazel got such a big bang out of Kellie's Aussie lingo. After a couple of small glasses of wine, the ladies were laughing and joking as though they had known each other for years. It was a great night and when they went back to Hazel's apartment for a cup of tea. Hazel asked them to stay there for the night. She said, "Then we can all go out and see the town tomorrow." Kellie wanted badly to stay, so it was all arranged and they stayed up and talked for hours.

At one point in the talk Hazel said, "Did you ever stop to wonder what would have happened if that turtle had not turned up when it did? Many times in my life things have turned up at the most astounding times. It was usually when I had given up all hope. I am firmly convinced that there must be a plan to our lives. What do you think, Kellie?"

Kellie thought for a minute, then said, "When I was in the canoe out in the middle of the ocean, I did a lot of thinking. Lots of times when it may have looked like I was sleeping, I was really thinking. I thought about Gordy, and the things he had done to get me away from Rabaul. He told me one very dangerous time, that he was the 'Brother of the Bear.' There was something looking after the big bozo, that was not hard to see. What Gordy believes seems to be working pretty well for him. I think maybe I'll go with his belief."

The next morning, Gordy took Kellie and Aunt Hazel out for breakfast. After making arrangements for the ferry trip to Prince Rupert the following morning, they went out to see the sights. Later on that same day Gordy took them all out to dinner again, then they went to a show. After the show they went back to Aunt Hazel's apartment. It was agreed by all that a nice cup of tea would hit the spot. When they were halfway thought their tea, Kellie asked, "Hazel, will you read our tea leaves? I really thought it was all malarkey at first, but he claims that you are really good at it." Hazel laughed, and said, "Gordon, what have you been telling this lovely young girl? We can sure have all the tea you want Kellie, but I can't read tea leaves, I never could."

Kellie glared at Gordy. "Gordon Cameron, you are a bounder! Do you know that! You deliberately told me a ruddy lie! For two cents I would bash you up! Do you know what this big, very funny bloke told me, Hazel? He told me that you read his tea leaves and said he was going to wake up in a hospital. The first woman he saw when he woke up, he would spend his life with. Have you ever heard such a pile of malarkey, I though it was malarkey when he told it to me, and I was right!"

Gordy laughed and said, "Well Kellie, I know beyond a shadow of a doubt that it is written down somewhere that you and I would meet. As Hazel said, it is all planned. Besides, when I woke up and saw that beautiful face and those big, soft brown eyes, I just knew I had to go back and try to get you home. I didn't wind up in your hospital by mistake, Kellie. Just like we did not get to that exact spot in the Coral Sea by accident, at the exact time the *Croydon* zigged instead of zagging. It was meant to be, I know it beyond a shadow of a doubt."

Gordy then said, "We had better turn in now. Tomorrow morning we catch the boat to Prince Rupert. Up the Inside Passage is one of the most spectacular trips in the world, and we want to be wide awake." Hazel and Kellie stayed up and talked for awhile, after Gordy went into the other room. Hazel had many questions that she wanted to ask Kellie, especially why she had stayed in Rabaul when she was sure the Japanese were coming. What had she thought when Gordy showed up to rescue her, and would she ever want to go back to see what happened after they left?

She said, "your parents must have worried an awful lot. I don't really know if I could have taken something like that, I'm sure. They must have been overjoyed when you finally contacted them." It was a good visit, and just what Hazel needed. She had enough stories to tell her elderly friends for the next six months.

After Kellie left her to go to bed, Hazel sat in her big easy chair and thought about how much she had enjoyed the day. Her husband Alvin had been wounded badly in the First World War, and although he had wanted to adopt a couple of kids, Hazel had been against it. Now she must fact life all alone, but she was so glad that Gordy was home with his new little wife. Hazel could no longer hold back the tears. The things she had not wanted when she was younger, seemed so precious now. She had thought then that they didn't have enough money to bring up a child. But as time went by, she had seen many people bring up kids on a lot less money than they had.

Chapter Thirteen

Dancing Lights

The boat trip up the inside passage from Vancouver to Prince Rupert was just as Gordy had said it would be, spectacular. The snow-covered mountains plunged from thousands of feet in the air, almost straight down into the sea. The ship seemed so small in comparison. All day they stood out on a deck, watching the panoramic view passing before them. Kellie was "cold as a billy goat," as she put it, but she didn't want to go inside and miss any of it. When they got off the ship at Prince Rupert, they were both excited. Gordy hired a water taxi at the same wharf to take them the rest of the way to Cedar Landing.

Two hours later they arrived in Cedar Landing, and it looked like the whole town was down on the wharf to welcome them. There was a big sign hung up on the dock saying WELCOME HOME GORDY. The whole population of the town was crowded onto the dock. His dad was there in the front row, along with his old friend Charley. Vera had stayed at home to cook up some goodies for the big welcome-home party that was going to be at Ed's house that night.

Everyone in town had read the story of how Gordy had gone back to Rabaul, to rescue Kellie. Ed had put it in the small local paper, so they all wanted to meet Kellie in the worst way. The party at Ed's house that night was a lively affair. The townsfolk ate and drank everything in the house and the music went on till the wee small hours of the morning. Just before Gordy and Kellie turned in for the night, Gordy borrowed a fur coat for Kellie and took her outside in the freezing, crisp night air. It was about ten below zero and clear as a bell that night. The northern lights were putting on a fantastic show. Kellie was spellbound at the mighty display. The lights seemed to bounce off the snow and everything sparkled like it was all brand new. The stars seemed so close, Kellie felt like she could almost touch them. She stood perfectly still and was speechless, it was though she had become hypnotized by the winter night's magic.

Three days later, Charley, Gordy, and Kellie went off into the winter wonderland. Charley had asked his friend Mr. Devereaux if he could use his cabin on the lake for a few days. They were very old friends so there was no problem. Besides, Charley had built the cabin for him a couple years before. It had snowed early that morning and everything looked like a Christmas card.

They put on snowshoes and borrowed some fur garments. "This is real Canadian," said Kellie. She had Vera take lots of pictures of her to send back to Aussie. Kellie had a hard time trying to walk fast in the snowshoes, so Gordy and Charley slowed down to a crawl. The quietness was haunting. The only noise was the crunch of the snowshoes in the snow. Although not a thing seemed to be there, Kellie felt that something was watching her all the time. Charley would stop once in a while to ask her, "Did you hear that noise?" Kellie would listen as hard as she could, but she never heard a thing. She would whisper to Gordy, "Did you hear anything?"

"Yes," said Gordy, "there is a bobcat over on that hill, under the cedar tree. He is just finishing his dinner. It was probably a rabbit." Kellie would look at him funny—she didn't know if he was pulling her leg or not. When they reached the log cabin by the lake, they went in and built a big fire in the stove. A cup of hot tea and something to eat made them feel refreshed. Then they all went down and stood on the shore of the lake. It was a picture that Kellie would never forget. Everything was so crystal clear, you could look across the lake and each tree stood out like it had been painted there.

That night after a big meal, they built a fire in the fireplace, drank tea, and talked for a long time. Charley wanted to know all about their escape from Rabaul. Gordy told Charley about the turtle that had its leg taken off by the Japanese destroyer. He told him how he had cooked it up, and said, "It tasted like that old piece of moose-meat we ate that time." Charley laughed, then he said, "Is it not strange, that it would be a three-legged turtle that saved your life? The Great Spirit will do strange things sometimes, to save a favorite hunter."

A few minutes later, Gordy said, "There was a time when Kellie and I were on our honeymoon at Apollo Bay. I woke up real early one morning because it was so hot, and I just couldn't get back to sleep. So I went out onto the small cottage veranda. The great expanse of Indian Ocean was as smooth as glass, and the sun was just coming up. I turned around and saw Kellie sleeping like a baby in the other room. Then I turned and looked out to the sea again. I said softly, 'Thank you so much for so much.' A minute later I felt a little puff of wind brush by my face, and I swear I heard a voice say, 'You're welcome.'"

Charley thought for a minute then he said, "Only the quiet heart can hear the soft voice of the Great Spirit. You have done well, my young friend."